The Prodigal
and
Other Stories

Luke Boyd

TotalRecall Publications, Inc.
1103 Middlecreek
Friendswood, Texas 77546
281-992-3131 TL

All rights reserved
ISBN: 978-1-59095-501-7
UPC: 6-43977-65013-9

Printed in the United States of America with simultaneous printings in Australia, Canada, and United Kingdom.

FIRST EDITION
1   2   3   4   5   6   7   8   9   10

For Sara
My wife of 64 years
for her love, support, and understanding

"A happy marriage
is a long conversation
which always seems
too short."
    --Andre Maurois

About the Author

Dr. Lucas G. "Luke" Boyd first saw the light of day in a three-room shot gun house on Jabe Dunnaway's place near Anguilla, Mississippi. Doc Smith, his uncle and country doctor, was the attending physician. It was the depths of the Depression. His father had lost his livelihood and had returned to the land to feed his family. However, within a few years, he was managing one of those sprawling, 2,000-plus acre cotton plantations The Delta was known for. This plantation culture of his early years left an indelible mark on his son.

A stroke of good fortune resulted in a scholarship to be one of the equipment managers for the football team, allowing him to attend The University of Mississippi, where he earned a B.S. degree. During his career he attended a total of five universities, two more of which saw fit to grant him degrees: Middle Tennessee State University (M.S.), The University of Tennessee (Ph.D. in English History.) Stints at The University of North Carolina and The University of Chattanooga were for special study in Economics and Far Eastern History, respectively.

He entered the Army through the ROTC program and served for two years as a 1st Lt. in an armored unit.

After leaving the service, he began a career in education which spanned 48 years both at the secondary and college levels. He retired after serving for 19 years as Principal of Battle Ground Academy, a private college preparatory school in Franklin, Tennessee.

His publishing credits include: four books, *Coon Dogs and Outhouses, Vol. I, Vol II,* and *Vol III; Don't Call Me Hero* (ghost writer), *The Story of a WW II Bomber Pilot; 9 short stories;* one article in the Tennessee Encyclopedia of History and Culture. He currently writes regular columns for a local newspaper, The Williamson Herald.

He and his wife, Sara, have been married for 64 years and have two children and two grandchildren. They live in Franklin, Tennessee.

He may be contacted via email at:
coondogspress@bellsouth.net.

Introduction

The first house I remember was a double pen structure which sat up on tall blocks. It was in the western part of The Delta not far from the Big River. The soil was buckshot which had only recently been released from the clutches of the surrounding swamp water. It was dark, grainy, and very rich but not easy to farm. When dry, it would shrink and develop large cracks. When wet, it was heavy, would clod up, and be very slick--some said, "as slick as owl shit." But in crop years when the weather was neither wet too late nor dry too early, it produced a bountiful harvest.

Light came from coal oil lamps. Water came from a pitcher pump in the back yard. There were no screens on the windows. There was an outhouse close by the garden fence. The road was dirt - mud when it rained. There were no books but there were always the stories.

My brother and I would not go to bed unless Daddy told us a story. I learned later that some were traditional fables. Others he just made up but they were all new to us.

My father was a story teller. There were many around. In a semi-literate society, that was the way family and community history was preserved. When my uncles came to visit, there were always sessions around the table after supper or on the front porch. I was always allowed to listen. Not only did I pick up a lot of information, I also learned how to tell a good story, a talent I have found useful throughout the years. At a book signing some years ago, a woman asked me what my philosophy of writing was. She was offended when I replied, "Ma'am, I'm just trying to tell a good story."

This pretty well parallels my wife Sara's assessment when I was asked what kind of writer I was. When I answered, "A Southern writer" they wanted to know what a Southern writer was. Sara broke in with, "That's someone who writes about nothing but still makes it interesting." So, I hope you readers find that at least some of the following stories not only to be "good stories," but also "interesting."

Now where did these fourteen tales come from? Some are true; some have an element of truth in them; four are chapters from a novel in progress; others just came into my mind and led me on a writing journey. But they are all fiction---more or less. That is not to say that some of these did not happen to some people at some time in some place. Nevertheless, they are still fiction.

Those who have read my earlier books probably noted that I tend to write in a light or humorous vein. Some of these pieces are just the opposite. One of my friends even accused me of "going over to the dark side." But a writer should be able to write about most anything as long as he/she "makes it interesting." Of course, you readers will be the judge of that.

Table of Contents

"The Prodigal"

"There's a land that is fairer than day,
And by faith we can see it afar."

The scratchy strains of "The Sweet By and By" came haltingly over the speakers in the Gilroy's Funeral Home and Chapel. Wilbur Gilroy hadn't bought a new record in over fifteen years, even though he'd gotten some complaints on the quality of his music. Complaints didn't move him. He was the only undertaker in Bent Tree, Alabama. If anybody wanted better music, let them bring their own at their expense.

"For the Father waits over the way,
to prepare us a dwelling place there."

The sound coming from the tin-can like speakers was uneven at best. Some of them had quit working and Wilbur reckoned as how he would have to call in Smokey Floyd from down at the radio shop if many more went out. Some of the funeral homes in bigger places were going to tape systems but Wilbur wasn't about to do something that expensive.

"In the sweet (in the sweet) by and by (by and by),
we shall meet on that beautiful shore; (by and by);"

Nelda Mae Cunningham's cheap casket sat at the front with the lid up. It was surrounded by a respectable number of flower arrangements. Some were beginning to wilt in the heat.

"In the sweet (in the sweet) by and by (by and by),
we shall meet on that beautiful shore."

All the windows were up and the back door was propped open

but the oppressive heat seemed to suck all the energy from the air, causing it to lay over everybody like a hot, humid comforter - felt but unseen. The hand-held fans fluttered in nearly everyone's hands, stirring the heavy air. Some said the advertising side with the big black printed letters and the color picture of the funeral home produced the best breeze; others swore that the side with the picture of the Last Supper gave more relief. Wilbur was proud of his fans. He had placed an ample supply in all the churches in town.

"We shall sing on that beautiful shore
the melodious songs of the blest."

The pews to the right of the small speaking platform were reserved for family members. Only two people sat there: Jessie Wayne Cunningham, Nelda Mae's second husband, and Lissie Sue Haycraft, a "friend" from the shirt factory, who had come to provide solace and comfort in Jessie Wayne's hour of bereavement.

"And our spirit shall sorrow no more,
not a sigh for the blessing of rest."

Jessie Wayne looked bored with the whole proceedings. He was a tall, lanky man whose limbs appeared to unfold when he rose to his feet. He had an angular face. Each feature seemed to be competing with its neighbor in some sharpness competition. He kept crossing and uncrossing his legs, revealing droopy socks and sharp shinbones.

"In the sweet (in the sweet) by and by (by and by),
we shall meet on that beautiful shore; (by and by);"

Lissie Sue was dressed all in black. Her short, tight dress struggled to contain her ample thighs and buttocks and exposed a considerable amount of flesh when she crossed her legs. Her shoes were pointy-toed stilettos and the broad-brimmed hat had a heavy veil that covered the top portion of her face. Her lower legs were encased in black, fish-net stockings which ended in wide elastic bands just above her knees. The little bowties woven within the mesh added a formal air to the outfit. She sat close to Jessie Wayne and patted him on the shoulder from time to time. She was aware of the condemning looks and the whispered comments among the other mourners. She seemed to be flaunting herself and the situation before them and daring them to do anything about it.

"In the sweet (in the sweet) by and by (by and by),
    we shall meet on that beautiful shore."

Brother Eustis Tutweiler, pastor of Bent Tree's First Southern Missionary Baptist Church, sat on the platform behind the pulpit mopping his florid face with a red bandana. He'd not preached a long sermon. He was new in town and hardly knew Nelda Mae. He was glad this was the last song.

"To our bountiful Father above,
    we will offer the tribute of praise"

As the third verse began, Wilbur and his assistant came forward, closed and locked the lid, and placed the pall on the casket. Suddenly, there came the sound of tires squealing on pavement and rocks being thrown aside by a car coming into the gravel parking lot at too great a speed. Next came the sound of the vehicle sliding to a stop and a car door slamming. All heads turned to the rear although the parking lot could not be seen from the chapel. Wilbur rushed out to see what was happening. The sound of angry voices came through the open door but the words were indistinguishable until the speakers got closer. Wilbur was heard to say, "But the casket has been locked," to which a strange voice replied, "I don't give a damn. If it can be locked it can surely be unlocked and if you won't do it, I will. Even if I have to break it open, I'm gonna see Mama one last time before you put her in the ground."

"For the glorious gift of his love,
and the blessings that hallow our days."

A tall man with a determined look on his face strode through the rear door. Wilbur trotted behind. A startled gasp went up from the mourners. Even though he was bald except for a dark ring of hair at ear level and even though they'd not seen him in years, most recognized Nelda Mae's son from her first marriage. Randall Lee Lattimore had finally come home. They began to whisper amongst themselves.

When they got to the front, Wilbur motioned for his assistant to help him remove the pall. Then he took the locking tool from his coat pocket and unlocked and raised the lid. Randall Lee stood looking down on his dead mother.

"In the sweet (in the sweet) by and by (by and by),
we shall meet on that beautiful shore (by and by).
In the sweet (in the sweet) by and by (by and by),
we shall meet on that beautiful shore."

As the song ended, the sounds of Wilbur's teenage son removing the record from the turntable came over the speakers. Randall Lee raised two fingers to his lips in a farewell kiss and then pressed them on his mother's cold lips. He stood at the casket for several minutes before going to the family area and seating himself on the far end of the pew occupied by his stepfather and "friend." For the first time he seemed to take note of Jessie Wayne. Their eyes met but no nod or other greeting passed between them.

Wilbur and his helper got the casket closed again and rolled it to the wide side doors where the hearse was backed up and waiting. The pall bearers put it into the vehicle. Wilbur came back inside and invited everyone to follow the hearse and family up the hill to the cemetery. Most did mainly because they were fascinated with this prodigal son who had returned after so many years.

As Randall Lee walked up the gravel drive behind the slow-moving hearse, he took out his handkerchief and mopped the sweat that was running off his bald head and down his face. He had forgotten just how hot summer could be in Alabama. Jessie Wayne and Lissie Sue fell into step beside him. Lissie Sue was having trouble maintaining her balance in the loose gravel with her high heels and clung tightly to Jessie Wayne's arm.

"How'd you find out?" Jessie Wayne hissed.

"I have ways," responded Randall Lee.

"You been gone so long you just shoulda stayed gone. Warn't no need in coming back now."

"That's not your problem," replied Randall Lee.

"Aren't you going to introduce us?" asked Lissie Sue as she fluttered her fake eyelashes behind the veil. One lash got caught in the mesh and she worked to free it.

"This is Randall Lee Lattimore, Nelda Mae's long lost son," said Jessie Wayne. There was sarcasm in his voice. And then turning to Randall Lee he said proudly, "This here's Lissie Sue Haycraft. She's a friend of mine from down at the shirt factory. She works in the office."

"So pleased to make your acquaintance," said Lissie Sue. Her lashes continued to flutter. Randall Lee just nodded.

"Looks like you could have spent a little more and gotten a

decent casket," Randall commented.

"Fancy boxes don't make no difference," retorted Jessie Wayne. "They're all going in the dirt and they're all gonna rot along with what's in 'em. No sense in paying extra."

"It's so gratifying to know that you're just as stingy as ever," said Randall Lee as he picked up his pace and left the two behind.

Most of the mourners crowded in under the shade of the canvas canopy that covered the gravesites. Reverend Tutweiler began delivering his final remarks. As Randall Lee sat in one of the folding chairs, his thoughts turned to the last time he'd seen his mother and the circumstances of his departure.

They had a good farm, a little over four hundred acres of good land. He and his daddy worked it with the help of their tenant, Barney Fowler. It was the fall of his senior year after the crops were in, when the tractor turned over and crushed the life out of his daddy. It wasn't long before Jessie Wayne began to come around. Randall Lee never liked him right from the start and told his mother so. "He's just after the farm, Mama," he'd tell her but she wouldn't listen. The next spring he and Barney had gotten the crops planted and he had graduated from high school. Jessie Wayne came for supper one night. After the meal, his mama broke the news.

"Jessie Wayne and I are gonna get married." Randall Lee sat dumbfounded. He tried to speak but couldn't. His mother continued, "Jessie Wayne thinks it's best that we rent the place out. He's got a good job at the shirt factory and running a farm is a lot of work."

Randall Lee found his voice. "But me and Barney can run the place. We've already got the crops planted and Jessie Wayne could help some."

"I ain't interested in helping," said Jessie Wayne. "I don't do farm work. We can sell off the livestock and equipment and make more on renting than we could farming it."

"But what about Barney?" asked Randall Lee. "He's been with us since before I was born."

"He'll just have to find himself another place." Jessie Wayne was uncompromising.

"Well, what about me?" Randall Lee asked. "This farm was what I'd planned on doing."

"You've finished school and you're eighteen now. It's time for you to make your own way," said Jessie Wayne.

His mother's silence told him that Jessie Wayne spoke for her as well but he turned to her in desperation.

"Where am I gonna make my own way, Mama? There's nothing for me to do in Bent Tree."

"Then you'll just hafta find another place." Jessie Wayne had spoken quickly before Nelda Mae could respond.

"We think it's best, dear," his mother replied. "You've got some money in your bank account and I can spare $500 to help you get started."

Randall Lee's whole body was numb. His world had collapsed around him. He wanted to smash in Jessie Wayne's smirking face but he controlled the urge. He got abruptly to his feet and went to his room before the two adults saw the hot tears that were running down his cheeks.

After Jessie Wayne left, she came to his room and handed him $500. He tried to reason with her but she wouldn't listen. The next morning he packed his clothes in a cardboard suitcase and left without saying goodbye. He drove the pickup into town and closed out his checking account. He parked the truck at the bus station and put the keys under the floor mat. Jessie Wayne could worry about getting it back to the farm. He bought a ticket and boarded the bus for Birmingham.

The loud "amen" brought him back to the present. Reverend Tutweiler offered syrupy words of condolence as he shook hands with Randall Lee, Jessie Wayne, and Lissie Sue. The service was over. As they got to their feet, Jessie Wayne turned to Randall Lee, "There's a sack of stuff at the house your mama wanted you to have. You can come by and pick it up sometime." He didn't wait for an answer but took Lissie Sue by the arm and headed back down the hill.

There was an awkward silence under the awning. Everyone seemed to be waiting for the next person to make the first move. From behind him came a voice, "Randall Lee, you turn around here and give me a hug." He turned and embraced the little white haired lady warmly.

"It's so good to see you, Mrs. Talley," he said. "Thanks for sending the telegram."

"It was the least I could do."

"But how'd you know where to find me?"

"We'll talk about all that later after supper tonight. You'll be staying with us just like you used to," said Mrs. Talley. Randall Lee started to protest but she would have none of it saying, "We've got some things we need to talk about. Now these folks want to speak to you," she said, sweeping one arm toward the crowd. His mother's long-time friends came around and shook his hand or hugged him. All said they were glad to see him back.

Finally, after everything had been said that could be said, the crowd gradually dispersed. He turned for one last look at his mother's grave. The grounds crew was shoveling in the dirt. It made a hollow sound as it hit her coffin. He and Mrs. Talley walked down the hill together. "How's Mr. Talley?" he asked.

"Oh, he's fine."

"Is he still at the post office?"

"Yes, he's the Post Master now."

"That's great. You said we needed to talk about something."

"Yes, we do. We'll do it after supper," said Mrs. Talley as she got into her car.

"I'm gonna drive around and look at all the changes in town. Then I'll be right on over," said Randall Lee.

There wasn't much new to see - a couple of new stores, some new paint, some new landscaping, a new fence and a new brick entrance to the shirt factory. As he drove, he couldn't help but think of Lester Ray Talley. They'd been best friends growing up, played ball together, been in Korea together but in different units. Lester Ray's unit had been in the front line with two ROK units on each side when the Chinese attacked. The two ROK units pulled out leaving Lester Ray's company out on a limb. They got cut off and suffered heavy casualties before a counter attack got through and rescued them. Lester Ray didn't make it. Every time he thought about it, Randall Lee got angry at those damned yellow-bellied Koreans for running off and getting his friend killed. He wondered how he was going to talk to Mr. and Mrs. Talley about Lester Ray. He had avoided saying anything at the cemetery because he didn't know what to say. He dreaded supper for that reason.

He parked in front of the Talley home and got his bag out of the trunk. Mrs. Talley met him at the door. "Come on down to your regular place," she said as she led him down the hall to Lester Ray's old room. Not much had changed in fifteen years.

The twin beds sat in the same place. It gave Randall Lee and eerie feeling. "I believe you always slept in that one," Mrs. Talley said pointing to the one on the left.

"Yes, that's right," acknowledged Randall Lee as he sat his bag down.

She put one arm around him. "It's so good to have you back. It's like a part of Lester Ray has come home. You remember all those nights you spent here after you all played in those late night ball games and all those weekends he spent with you hunting and fishing on your farm? We all had some wonderful times together. I still miss him so much." Mrs. Talley pulled up the corner of her apron and dabbed her eyes.

"Of course I remember," replied Randall Lee. "Those kinds of things you don't forget. You were a second mama to me."

She put both arms around him and hugged him tightly for a long moment. Finally, she dropped her arms and said, "That's enough of this. We can't live in the past. Let's just be happy right now. I'm going down and finish up supper. You freshen up and get those traveling clothes off and into something comfortable. Then come on down to the kitchen." She left still wiping her eyes on her apron.

As Randall Lee was washing up, he heard Mr. Talley come in. He changed into jeans and a t-shirt and headed for the rear of the house. Mr. Talley greeted him warmly, pumping his hand and slapping him on the shoulder. "Boy, you've turned into a fine looking man. But what have you done with your hair?" Mr. Talley always liked to tease about something.

"I left it in Korea."

"I didn't know they were still taking scalps in that war."

"They weren't. I think my scalp froze one night up by The

Chosen Reservoir. Hair began to come out in hunks and never grew back. I'm just glad it wasn't my feet. Say, since you've brought it up, looks like the same thing has happened to you," said Randall Lee as he rubbed a hand over the older man's shiny pate. They both laughed.

"I see you two haven't forgot how to needle each other," said Mrs. Talley. "Now come on to the table before the food gets cold." They sat down to a sumptuous meal.

After they had helped their plates, Mr. Talley asked, "Okay, how about giving us a sketch of what you've been doing since you left?"

"Well," Randall Lee replied, "I went to Birmingham and got a job in one of the steel mills. After a few months, I decided I didn't want to do that the rest of my life so I got accepted at the Police Academy, graduated, and started with the Birmingham Police Department. I'd also joined the National Guard and when the Korean War broke out, we got called up. You all knew Lester Ray and I ran into each other there. Anyway, we had done some training at Camp Carson, Colorado, and I sort of liked it out there, so when I got back, I got on with the Denver Police Department. They have a program where you can go to school along with the police work so I used my G.I. Bill, went to class at night and on weekends and got a degree in Criminal Justice. I'm a Detective now and do a lot of undercover work. But changing the subject, how in the world did you know how to reach me?"

"We'll go into all of that later," replied Mrs. Talley. Randall Lee's detective's antenna was beginning to pick up some vibrations. Something wasn't right - it didn't exactly fit together. He wondered what it was.

After finishing off a large helping of homemade peach

cobbler, Randall Lee got up and began to clean the table. "Remember, this used to be my job," he said, "and then Lester Ray and I'd do the dishes."

"Yes. And you all always argued over whose turn it was to dry," replied Mrs. Talley. She hugged him again. "Those were wonderful days. But let's just put these in the sink and run some water over them. We'll go into the den and talk."

After they were seated there was an awkward silence. Finally, Mrs. Talley spoke. "We're so sorry, Randall Lee. If we had just done something, your mama would still be alive."

"What in the world do you mean?" asked Randall Lee.

"When's the last time you heard from your mama?" Mrs. Talley asked.

"Pretty soon after I got to Denver. Her letters just quit coming. I tried to call her a couple of times but the phone was no longer in service. But I never quit writing. I just hoped she'd want to talk to me again or see me."

Mr. Talley spoke up. "I know you never quit writing to her but she thought you did and we also know that she never quit trying to contact you."

"How do you know this? What could have happened to the letters?" Randall Lee's detective mind was racing.

"Because I kept seeing your letters come through the post office. We don't get much first class mail from Denver. Of course, all I could do was put them in the mailbox. It was about that time that Jessie Wayne took the mailbox down at the farm and rented a post office box. He always picked up the mail. He also had the phone taken out and sold the car. She was just isolated out there. Jessie Wayne didn't let her go any place unless he took her in his pickup and stayed right with her." He turned to his wife.

"Honey, tell him what Nelda Mae told you at the grocery that day."

"Well, Jessie Wayne was back at the meat counter when I ran into Nelda down one of the aisles. She seemed desperate to talk. Said she didn't know why you'd quit writing to her, that she was still writing to you hoping you'd forgive her and write. I knew right then something wasn't right. The only way she had to mail them was to send them by Jessie Wayne. He had to be short-stopping them and not bringing your letters to her. Before I could think of what to say or whether I should say anything, Jessie Wayne came up and took her away. Oh, she also said that Jessie was the biggest mistake she'd ever made."

"That sorry bastard," said Randall Lee. "Pardon my language."

"That's okay. We feel the same way," said Mr. Talley.

"But that's not the worst part," replied Mrs. Talley. "We just shoulda done something when the other came up."

"What other?" queried Randall Lee.

"Well, you know I've been working in old Doc Stone's office for years. About three months ago your mama began to come in with stomach problems. Doc couldn't figure out what the problem was. A couple of weeks ago she was in for a visit with Jessie Wayne out in the waiting room. The nurse came out and whispered to me that Nelda wanted to see me back in the examination room. I went back and she said that she was sure Jessie Wayne was poisoning her. I asked her if she'd told Doc and she said she had but that he just told her it was her imagination. I suggested she go to another doctor but she said that Doc Stone was the contract doctor for the shirt factory and that Jessie Wayne wouldn't take her anywhere else. We didn't know what to do.

We'd about decided that we were going to contact you since we had your address from your letters but we'd waited too long. Last Tuesday Jessie Wayne said he came in from work and found her dead in the kitchen floor."

"Doesn't the law require an autopsy in deaths like this?" asked Randall Lee.

"Yes, it does," replied Mr. Talley, "But Doc Stone is the county coroner and since he'd been treating her, he said one wasn't necessary."

"What did he list as the cause of death?" asked Randall Lee.

"Complications," answered Mrs. Talley, "I typed up the death certificate."

"Good Lord," responded Randall Lee. "This is beginning to seem like a bad dream. Who's the Sherriff these days?"

"Jack Dell Lipsey," answered Mr. Talley. "You probably remember him."

"Yeah. He was a ding-a-ling deputy when I was in high school. How in the world did he get elected?"

"J. Kimber Britton backed him," said Mr. Talley.

"He still own the shirt factory?"

"Yes. And several more around in other towns."

"He still pretty much run the town?"

"Yes. And he's the Mayor now. I guess he got tired of just running things and wanted the title, too," answered Mr. Talley.

"What's Jessie Wayne do down there now?"

"Oh, he's one of the big supervisors."

"How long's he been messing around with this Lissie Sue person?"

"Oh, I guess about eight or nine months now," answered Mrs. Talley. "He picks her up most every morning and they have breakfast together at Boonie Mae's Café. He takes her on to work and back home in the afternoon. The neighbors say that sometimes he lingers awhile."

"I'll bet he does," said Randall Lee. He got up and walked out on the back porch and stood leaning against a post looking at nothing in particular. He was running everything through his mind. He could easily put all the pieces together but proof would be a hard thing to come by and he could probably not expect any help from local law enforcement. What he needed was a good plan. He began to search for one in his head.

Mr. Talley walked out on the porch. "What do you think?" he asked.

"Well, first off I thought I'd just go out and kill the sombitch but I've rejected that idea. I don't know exactly what I'm gonna do but I know one thing, that bastard is not gonna get away with this." Mr. Talley went back inside and left Randall Lee to his thoughts.

He didn't sleep much that night. He kept coming up with ideas and then rejecting them. By morning he had the nucleus of a plan.

After breakfast he drove out to the farm. As he turned down the long lane that led to the house, he couldn't help but notice how shabby and overgrown the place was.

His daddy always kept the place mowed and looking good. Barney's house was all grown up in weeds as was the barn lot and all the outbuildings. The only thing kept up was the fenced yard of the main house. Since it was Saturday, Randall Lee figured Jessie Wayne would be home but no one was about. He parked his car, went through the front gate and walked around the yard. His mother would have been ashamed of the way the place looked. As he stood contemplating his next move, he heard a vehicle coming up the lane. Jessie Wayne parked his pickup by Randall Lee's car and he and Lissie Sue got out. "I see you're out here snooping around," was Jessie Wayne's greeting.

Randall Lee ignored the accusation. "You said you had something for me. I came to see about it."

"I'll get it," said Jessie Wayne as he headed for the house leaving Lissie Sue with Randall Lee. She tried to flutter her eyelashes but without the false ones she'd had on at the funeral, there was not much to flutter.

"I've come to check out the house - to see just how much redecorating I'm gonna have to do before I move in. Of course, I'll wait a reasonable amount of time."

"It's good to see that Jessie Wayne has taken up with someone who has such a wonderful social awareness," replied Randall Lee sarcastically.

Jessie Wayne came out of the house carrying a brown grocery bag from the Pack-N-Sack Market. He handed it to Randall Lee. "Yore mama wanted you to have this stuff. I don't want it ever said that I didn't honor the wishes of the dead."

"You're all heart," said Randall Lee as he looked inside the sack. It was about half full of loose pictures and a couple of old photo albums just thrown into the sack helter-skelter. He decided to bait Jessie Wayne a little.

"Is this all?"

"Of course, that's all. What more would there be?"

"I thought maybe she'd leave me part of the farm?"

Jessie Wayne snorted like a bull getting ready to charge. "Part of the farm! You've got your nerve. You leave and stay gone fifteen years and expect to get something? My name's on the deed now and all this is mine. You ain't got nothing else coming so it ain't no reason for you to be on my property after this. If you do come about, I'll call the Sherriff on you and have you arrested for trespassing. Now, get off my place."

Randall Lee resisted the urge to give Jessie Wayne the beating he deserved. He would find another way. He looked at him a long moment through narrowed eyes. Jessie Wayne began to get nervous as he realized the precarious position he'd put himself into. Finally, Randall Lee turned to Lissie Sue, "Miss Haycraft, I'd be mighty careful if I were you. When you move in with this man, you ought to think about eating most of your meals out."

With that he turned on his heel, strode through the front gate,and got in his car, leaving Jessie Wayne and Lissie Sue to wonder just how much he knew.

He drove toward town until he found a small stand of pine beside the road. He pulled over into their shade and set about examining the contents of the sack. It was obvious that Jessie Wayne had gone through everything and just thrown it in the sack. His mother would have been neat and careful. He had the distinct feeling that she was trying to tell him something. The question was,"was she smart enough to get a message past Jessie Wayne and was he smart enough to find it?" His detective training took over as he began to examine the sack's contents.

The photos were mostly black and white - the ones he remembered growing up. There he was at various ages, his parents as well, pictures of the farm, pictures of him and Lester Ray with a big string of fish or a limit of squirrels. There were two or three of his mother with Jessie Wayne. He was tempted to tear them up but set them aside. There were two old black photo albums. Most of the loose pictures had come from these. The ones remaining in the books had at least two of their corners pulled up. Jessie Wayne had made sure that there were no messages hidden behind any of the pictures.

At the bottom of the bag was his mother's Bible, King James Version. It was bound in black leather with gold lettering and showed signs of heavy use. Randall Lee picked it up and leafed through it. There were a couple of bookmarks but nothing else. He fluttered the pages one last time and started to put it back in the sack - but for some reason it just didn't feel right. He examined it more closely, trying to figure out what had caught his attention. He soon figured out that the back cover was much stiffer than the front cover. He saw why. The first page past the front cover was of very heavy black material, which gave support to the leather cover. There was one at the back as well but it was stuck to the back cover making it much stiffer. Closer examination revealed that it had been glued down along the edges. Randall Lee took out his knife and popped the glue loose. A folded sheet of paper was inside.

His heart began to race. His hands were shaking so hard that he could hardly unfold the sheet. Finally, he got it done and read:

> *Dear Randall Lee,*
> *If you are reading this, I'll be dead. Jessie Wayne is poisoning me and I don't know how to get away from him. He's got a new girlfriend and his name's now on the deed to the farm. Soon he'll   have everything and I'll be gone. Please don't let him get away with this.*
> *The two worst mistakes of my life were*

*marrying him and letting him run you off. I
hope you can   forgive me. I never stopped
trying to get in touch with you and I've never
stopped loving you.*

All my love,

Mama

Randall Lee wiped the tears out of his eyes and read the short letter again. A raging fire burned inside him. His first impulse was to get his service revolver out of the trunk and go back and shoot both Jessie Wayne and Lissie Sue. But then he didn't know for sure that Lissie Sue was in on it. He suspected that she was but he couldn't say just yet. He leaned back in the seat to try to get control of his emotions. He thought of his mother like a trapped animal waiting to be slaughtered. The words came out loud, "No, Mama, he's not going to get away with it."

After a few minutes, he began to think like a detective. Where would Jessie Wayne get the poison? He'd have to sign for it wherever he went. He'd probably not used either of the two drug stores in Bent Tree. He'd go some place where he wasn't known, probably Selma. It was only 27 miles away. He started the car and headed for Selma.

As he hit the town's outskirts, he slowed down and began looking for a drug store. Considering how lazy Jessie Wayne was, he doubted he'd drive to the other side of the town. Save-a-Lot Drugs was his first stop. He parked and took one of the photos of his mother and Jessie Wayne in with him. He waited until the pharmacist finished up with a customer and then walked up to the counter in an authoritative manner. He flashed his badge being careful that the pharmacist didn't see that it was from

Denver. "My name's Perkins," he said. "I'm helping with an investigation we've got going on in Bent Tree. Have you ever seen this man before?"

The pharmacist studied the picture for several seconds. "Yes. He has been in."

"Would you happen to remember any specific purchase he made?"

"Yes. He bought arsenic."

Randall Lee couldn't believe his good fortune but he pressed on just to make sure. "Are you sure about that? After all you only saw him once and you can remember him and what he bought?"

"Well actually, he came in twice. Bought arsenic both times. I don't sell much poison so those sales sort of stick with me. Said he wanted to kill some rats. I asked him why he didn't buy it over in Bent Tree and he said that he was here on some other business so it was just convenient. This woman wasn't with him though."

"No. She wouldn't have been," said Randall Lee.

"But he did have a woman with him the second time."

"Can you describe her?"

"Well, she was sort of trashy looking. She fluttered her eyelashes a lot. The only thing she said was, 'Be sure to get enough this time to kill all the rats.'"

So Miss Lissie Sue was a partner in the crime. "Did you have him sign for it?"

"Of course I did. Let me get the book out of the safe." He soon reappeared with a black ledger. It didn't take long for him to locate the entries. "Here they are," he said as he placed the book on the counter and pointed to the two lines. "And that's his driver's license number." Jessie Wayne's signatures were bold and clear. Randall Lee noted the dates in his little notebook.

"If we go to trial, we may have to subpoena these records."

"You won't have to. They're public records. Just have the DA send an official request and I'll send a certified copy."

"What about testifying?" asked Randall Lee.

"I'll be glad to. Just need to know where and when."

Randall Lee thanked the pharmacist for his help and took his leave. He located a drive-in and ate a sandwich. Everything was falling into place but all the evidence was circumstantial. Several plans kept running through his head.

When he got back to Bent Tree, he went over his latest discoveries with the Talleys and spent the remainder of the day sitting out on their back porch in a rocking chair deep in thought.

He attended church with the Talleys the next morning. Brother Tutweiler was not a dynamic preacher and even less so when most of his words were drowned out by the two large window fans. After the service a number of people came by to speak to him - several he'd gone to school with and they all seemed glad to see him.

Mrs. Talley prepared one of her patented Sunday dinners - fried chicken with all the trimmings. Randall Lee realized that even though he liked the West, there were just some things he couldn't get in Colorado.

After helping clean the dishes, he asked Mr. Talley, "Where does Jack Dell live?"

"In the old Tate house."

"Well, he's come up a little from the trailer park."

"Yes, he has. But surely you're not going to see him today."

"Surely, I am. There's no sense in wasting an afternoon."

"Frankly, I don't think you're going to get much help from him."

"Maybe not. But I'm in law enforcement and I believe these things ought to be taken care of by the local agencies - or at least they should be given the opportunity. And that's what I'm gonna do - give Jack Dell the opportunity."

"Well, I wish you luck," said Mr. Talley.

Randall Lee parked in front of Jack Dell's house. Jack Dell was sitting on the front porch, wearing an old pair of jeans and a white, strap undershirt. He was bare footed. An extension cord snaked out under one of the front window screens to provide power to the oscillating fan that stirred the humid air around him. He was drinking a beer.

Randall Lee walked up to the porch and said, "I'm Rand…"

Jack Dell cut him off. "I know who you are."

"Well, that's good. I need to talk to you about something."

"Then come down to the office in the morning."

Randall Lee's eyes narrowed. When he spoke again there was an edge in his voice. "You're the Sheriff and you know as well as I do that Sherriff's don't have banker's hours. You need to know something and I intend to tell you right now." As he talked, he walked up on the porch and sat down in a chair opposite Jack Dell.

Jack Dell seemed a little startled by his forcefulness. "Well, talk then," he said, taking a swig of his beer.

"You've got a local homicide that needs investigating."

"First I've heard of it. Who's the victim?"

"My mother."

"Doc Stone didn't seem to think so."

"That's because he didn't do an autopsy. Let me tell you what I've found out." Randall Lee laid everything out -his mother's fears, her stomach problems, the way Jessie Wayne had isolated her, Jessie Wayne's new girl friend and his purchases of arsenic in Selma.

"That's all very interesting, but that don't prove murder."

"You're right, but that's enough to get an order to exhume and do an autopsy. She's gonna be full of poison. And if she's not, that's the end of it."

Jack Dell took several swallows of beer before answering. "That's too much trouble. I'm awful busy this summer."

"I could help you with the investigation. I've been a detective for…."

"That's the last thing I need," Jack Dell broke in, "some big city detective trying to tell me what to do. No, thank you. And I done told you, I'm busy."

Randall Lee was about to reach the end of his patience. "Busy with what?"

"Busy with all them damned freedom riders, that's what." Jack Dell's voice began to rise. "Maybe you ain't got the word in Denver, but they're all over the place around here. Been coming through here ever few days on they way to Selma and Montgomery."

"Do they get off the bus?" asked Randall Lee.

"They hasn't yet, but you never know what might happen. I gotta be a'settin' on ready at all times. What would happen if some got off one day and tried to integrate The Bus Stop Café? Why, there'd be hell to pay. I've requested some police dogs just in case but I think Bull Conner's got them all spoke for. So, that's what I'm busy with, Mister Big City Detective. What you need to do is get you a calendar and a map. This is 1963 and this is Alabama. We do what we damn well please around here."

"And it doesn't please you to look into my mother's murder?"

"Naw, it don't. Especially since I don't know it was one."

"And you're not gonna know because you're not going to do any basic investigating to find out." Randall Lee got to his feet. "But I want you to mark this down: when something bad happens down the road, I gave you a chance to get ahead of the curve and you didn't take it." With that he stomped off the porch and went to his car, leaving Jack Dell Lipsey sucking on his beer and with the breeze from the fan flapping the tattered cuffs of his pants.

***

"I'm not gonna say, 'I told you so,'" said Mr. Talley.

"You don't have to," replied Randall Lee. "I pretty well knew I was shooting in the dark but I had to give it a try."

"What's next?" asked Mrs. Talley.

"I guess I'll just have to go with Plan B."

"What's that?" she wanted to know.

"I haven't figured that all out just yet. I'll have to do some more studying on it."

The Talley's looked at each other. It was obvious they'd been discussing the matter. Mr. Talley fixed him with a penetrating gaze before speaking. "We've been talking about this. We've lost one son and we don't want to lose another. We know you're a grown man now but we want you to promise us that you won't go and do something foolish and have to spend the rest of your life in prison or worse. Will you promise?"

Randall Lee took both their hands in his before speaking. "You have my word on that. If I was gonna do something stupid, I would have already done it." The Talleys seemed relieved. "But I'm telling you, those two are going to pay. I've just got to figure out how to get it done. You know Mama always said that there was more than one way to skin a cat. I'm just looking for that other way." They both hugged him real tight. He spent the rest of the afternoon in the rocking chair on the back porch, lost in thought.

They had just sat down to supper when there was a knock at the front door. Mrs. Talley answered it and came back saying, "Someone wants to see you, Randall Lee. He's waiting on the porch."

As Randall Lee walked out the front door, he saw a big man wearing some sort of security uniform. He had a large beer gut and carried a pistol on his hip. The nametag said his name was Frank. "I've got a message for you," he said.

"Who's it from?"

"It's from the man who runs things around here."

"And just who might that be?"

"If you don't know that, you ain't got enough sense to walk around good."

"Well, what is it?"

"You listen careful 'cause I ain't gonna repeat it. The Boss says for you to leave Jessie Wayne Cunningham alone. He's a good man. We don't need any of you big city folks helping us run things around here, so you'd best just head on back out West where you belong." With the message delivered, Frank stalked out to his pickup, which bore the shirt factory name and logo on the door. Randall Lee watched him go without responding.

Back at the table he related the latest development to the Talleys ending with, "It didn't take ole Jack Dell long to get the word to Britton."

"I'm not surprised," replied Mr. Talley. "Everybody in

government, both city and county, is in his pocket. If you're not, you don't have a job. And another thing my boy, if you keep on poking around, you're gonna stir up a hornet's nest."

"Then, I guess I'll just have to do it without poking too much."

***

After breakfast the next morning, Randall Lee drove by the shirt factory to make sure Jessie Wayne's pick up was in the parking lot. Then, he drove around town a couple of times just to make sure Jack Dell didn't have a deputy on his tail. Seeing nothing, he left town in the opposite direction of the farm. After a few miles, he turned off on a back road and turned on several more of the same until he came out on the main road about two miles beyond the farm. As he approached the lane, his sharp eye caught the reflection from the glass of a vehicle coming from the house. He pulled over behind a clump of bushes and watched. Soon, a patrol car pulled out of the road and turned toward town. It only went about a half mile before stopping and backing into a blind lane, which led to another farm. Randall Lee doubted they were looking for speeders. He was their target. He backed up the way he'd come until he could turn around. Then, he went back about three quarters of a mile hoping he could locate the old trail that ran between the two farms. Since it ran mostly down through pine woods, it probably wasn't too overgrown. He managed to locate it and found it still passable. After a ways he parked under some small pines and got out. .He walked up through the trees to a hay field and on across it to a fence row which ran beside the main house.

He stood hidden by the fence row for several minutes, surveying the house. He didn't think they would leave a deputy there. They knew he'd come by car so they were probably both with the patrol car out on the main road. But he wanted to be as sure as possible. Seeing no sign of life, he climbed the fence and went up into the yard.

There was no one about. The front door was locked as was the back but getting in wasn't a problem. He went to their secret "get in" side door, took out his pocketknife and popped the Yale night latch. He walked around inside being careful not to disturb anything. Most of the house was still neat except for the unmade bed and the dishes in the sink. The rest of the dishes were clean and stacked in the cabinets. One cabinet held Jessie Wayne's liquor supply - two bottles of Scotch and four of assorted bourbons. It had to be his. His mother didn't drink.

He kept a wary eye and ear out should the patrol car return. He could easily hide if they did. They did not expect him to come in on foot.

Jessie Wayne had been doing some paper work at the kitchen table. There were papers and other stuff scattered about on it. A wastebasket sat nearby containing some of the discards. Randall Lee looked through it and selected two pages, which were almost full of Jessie Wayne's writings. He also found several cancelled checks with Jessie Wayne's signature. He selected one, folded it in with the pages, and slipped them into his pocket.

He did not do a thorough search of the house because he concluded that Jessie Wayne probably would not hide the stuff where his mother might find it. That left the outside. He went out the back door locking it behind him. Stopping at the back gate, he surveyed the big barn and several outbuildings. It would take several men several days to go over everything. He resigned himself to the fact that he wasn't going to find the arsenic. Jessie

Wayne may even have disposed of the leftovers.

Standing there leaning on the gate, Randall Lee was embarrassed at how unkempt everything was. Only the yard inside the fence was mowed. The rest of the area was high weeds. Then suddenly, he saw it. There was a path starting just outside the gate and leading towards the barn. He knew his mother wouldn't have made it and what reason would Jessie Wayne have for going to an abandoned barn? He followed the path down through the open barn gate, through the barn lot and up to one of the doors. The pressed down weeds indicated that the door had been opened recently. He went in and saw that there was a distinct path in the loose dirt, which led up to the door to the tack room. His heart sank when he saw the heavy chain and padlock securing the door.

He stood trying to figure out a solution. He could take the door off its hinge but that would take some tools he didn't have and leave some marks he didn't want to leave. It soon occurred to him that as lazy as Jessie Wayne was, he'd probably hide a key around the barn someplace. However, there were no paths in the dirt anyplace else. As he looked around he noted that everything was covered in dust except for a small place near the top of a two by eight support beam, which ran between the main roof supports. He felt up on top of the beam and found the key.

The first thing that caught his eye when he opened the door was the large cotton basket sitting over to one side. It was over half full of letters. He bent over and looked closely. There were all the letters he'd written his mother and all the letters she'd written to him -all unopened. Hot anger welled up in his chest. If Jessie Wayne had been present, he would have beaten him to death on the spot.

The rest of the room was almost bare. There were a few pieces of harness rotting on pegs along one wall. The old medicine cabinet still hung on the back wall. He turned the latch and opened the double doors. There, still on the shelves were all the old liniments and medicines his daddy had used to doctor the farm animals. As he stood looking at the old bottles and cans, something caught his eye - something unusually white almost hidden behind a bottle of Jensen violet. He reached back and gingerly plucked out a container from Save-a-Lot Drugs. There was a skull and cross bones on all four corners of the label with "arsenic" printed in bold letters. There was still plenty left.

Randall Lee put it back in its place and retraced his steps, locking everything and making sure everything was just as he had found it. He went back to his car and drove back to town the round-about way he had come.

When he got to Bent Tree, he drove up to the main highway and stopped in front of a concrete block building. The sign on the front read:

The Ledger

The Citizens' Newspaper

Lynn Larson, Jr., Owner & Editor

Lynn had been about three years ahead of him in school so they had only known each other casually. Lynn's father had founded the paper and Lynn had grown up in the business.

Randall Lee went in. The building had no interior walls and was filled with all sorts of printing machines. One was clacking away in the back as two men worked on some printing project. Lynn and a woman were hovering over a big table working on lay-out. Randall Lee started to introduce himself but Lynn cut him off with, "I know who you are. It's good to have you back in town." They shook hands. "What can I do for you?"

"I'd like to talk to you about something."

"Sure. Just come over to my office." Lynn led him over to one front corner where a five-foot partition had been erected. The desk and a couple of tables were covered with all manner of newspaper stuff. He motioned Randall Lee to a chair. Their voices wouldn't carry very far over the noise of the machine.

"Has your dad retired?"

"In a manner of speaking. He died about five years ago."

"I'm sorry."

"That's okay. You didn't know."

"As I remember your father was a straight shooter. He used to write editorials against J. Kimber Britton and the way he was taking over the town. What I want to know is are you anything like your daddy?"

Lynn studied Randall Lee for a long moment before answering. "I'd like to think I'm just like him. This paper supports honest candidates for office and points out Britton's policies that enrich him and cost the city and county dearly. But he's too powerful and I can't see that I'm making much of a dent. He'd like to see me go under. The shirt factory has more printing jobs than any business in town and Britton sends them all to Birmingham even though I could do them better and cheaper. Same thing with the city and county printing jobs. I'm barely hanging on but I'm still hanging. But why does this concern you?"

"Because I've got a story that Britton and some of his folks want to keep quiet. When it breaks, it's going to need some publicity by somebody who's not afraid of bucking them. I'm just trying to determine if you're that somebody."

Lynn looked around to make sure no one was within earshot, picked up a notepad and said, "I'm your man. Lay it on me."

"There's been a murder and those in control don't want to admit it."

"Who?"

"My mother."

"Are you serious?"

"I'm dead serious. And I'm gonna tell you everything I know and how I found it out so when the thing breaks, you won't have to go scratching around for stuff." Randall Lee then proceeded to lay everything out, omitting none of the details.

Lynn sat for a moment in amazement. "Does anybody else know about this?" he asked.

"The Talleys know everything. Jack Dell knows everything except the letters and that I found the poison. The Talleys will keep it quiet and Jack Dell's not about to go stirring up anything."

"When and how are we going to break the story?" asked Lynn.

"What I want you to do is be a good newspaperman and sit on this for the time being. All I can say is when it comes time to break it, you'll know it without me saying anything to you. I need for you to trust me like I'm trusting you. Can we leave it that way?"

"We sure can."

"Okay. I've got to get back to Denver right now but something is going to happen pretty soon."

"I'll be waiting." The two men shook hands.

Randall Lee drove to the Talleys, went straight to his room, and started packing his suitcase. He was surprised when he heard Mrs. Talley come out of the kitchen. "I thought you'd be at Doc Stone's," he said. "I was just going to leave you a note."

"I don't work Monday and Tuesday. Has something happened?"

"No, I just need to get back to Denver for right now."

"Have you had any lunch?"

"No, I'll just grab a sandwich on my way out of town."

"No you won't. I'll fix you a sandwich with a big glass of tea while you finish packing. It won't take any longer."

As he ate, he told her about finding the letters and the arsenic. "Of course," he said, "you can tell Mr. Talley but please don't breathe a word of this to anybody else. I'm working on something and if word gets out, everything will blow up."

"You can count on us," she said.

When he finished eating, she gave him a long hug before letting him go.

***

He returned the rental car where he'd picked it up near the Birmingham airport and was standing at the counter finishing up the paperwork. "I hope you found everything satisfactory," said the rental agent.

"Yes, everything was fine."

"Are you catching a flight?"

"Yes, I've got to get back to Denver."

"You can catch one of our shuttles out front next to the taxi stand. They run every fifteen minutes and will take you straight to the main terminal. Hope you have a good flight home."

Randall Lee thanked the man and went to a bank of payphones in the lobby where he made several calls. He then walked out the front door and down toward the taxi stand and shuttle stop.

***

Jessie Wayne had picked up Lissie Sue and they were in their regular booth by the front window of Boonie Mae's Café having breakfast before heading for their jobs at the shirt factory. "It's hard to believe that Nelda Mae's been dead a little over two weeks now and ever thing is going good," said Jessie Wayne.

Lissie Sue reached across the table and put her hand on his arm before speaking. "I told you it would. All we've gotta do is just sit tight."

"Yeah, I'm sure you're right," he responded. "Randall Lee tried to stir up some dust but he's gone back out West now with his tail between his legs."

"What did I tell you?" she replied. "Ole J. Kimber's gonna take care of us. We're valuable employees."

"I'm glad of that," said Jessie Wayne. "And you know I've been thinking over what you said. We ought to sell off the farm and I move into town with you. We could take the few nice things from the house and auction the rest."

"I'm glad you're seeing that now, Honey," responded Lissie Sue. "It'd be a lot more convenient and we wouldn't be tied down by that land in case we need to go somewhere in a hurry."

Just then a rather beat up pick-up pulled in and parked near the front door. It was two-tone- maroon and cream - and not local. Jessie Wayne had never seen it around. A tall, bushy haired man got out carrying a black, canvas rucksack. He had a scruffy beard and wore a John Deere cap and dark sunglasses - the kind where the wearer's eyes are not visible. His well-worn denim work shirt and pants and the scuffed up work shoes marked him as some type of laborer, probably just passing through to another job. He came in and selected a table in the far corner. He removed his cap but not the glasses. After the waitress brought him a cup of coffee and took his order, he fetched a newspaper out of the rucksack and began to read it as he sipped the coffee. Jessie Wayne noticed that no matter how the man held the paper, those sun-glassed eyes were always visible. Jessie Wayne began to feel as if the man were watching them. It gave him an uneasy feeling. He leaned into Lissie Sue.

"I think that man is watching us."

Lissie Sue cut her eyes in the man's direction. "I think he's reading the paper," she said.

"Well, for some reason I don't feel easy about him," said Jessie Wayne.

The man's order came and he began to eat while still reading the paper. Jessie Wayne and Lissie Sue finished, paid their tab and headed out for work. The man in the corner continued to eat and read.

About an hour later, Lissie Sue was at her desk. The little sign beside her door said, "Personnel Office." The receptionist buzzed her on the intercom and said, "There's a gentleman here who wants to fill out an application."

"Send him on in," she replied as she turned her chair around to put a folder in a file cabinet behind her desk. When she turned back around, she almost screamed. Standing in front of her desk was the bushy haired man holding his cap in one hand and the rucksack in the other. The glasses were still on. He gave no indication of noticing her reaction.

"I'd like to put in an application, ma'am," he said.

"I...I... I don't think we'll be hiring any time soon," she stammered.

"That's okay. I've got time and you never know what might

turn up."

"I guess that's right. You never know," she said nervously. She took an application form from her desk and handed it to him. "You can sit here," she said indicating a wooden tablet armchair next to her desk. "Are you new around there?"

"Yes," he replied as he sat down and began filling out the form. The sun glasses stayed on.

"Would you like some coffee or a Coke?" Lissie Sue offered.

"A Coke could be nice," he said.

As soon as she was out of the office, he stood up and reached around and began pulling open drawers until he found the letterhead stationery. He took several sheets and slipped them into his bag. When she returned, he thanked her for the Coke and sipped on it as he finished the form. He handed it to her. thanked her again, and took his leave. Lissie Sue felt a sense of relief. For some reason just the stranger's presence intimidated her.

As they ate lunch together in the factory cafeteria, Lissie Sue told Jessie Wayne about the man coming in and filling out an application. "Did you check it out?" he asked.

"I've been too busy this morning but I'm going to this afternoon."

About mid-afternoon Lissie Sue sent word for Jessie Wayne to come to her office. "Nothing checks out," she said.

"Are you sure?"

"Of course, I'm sure. And I mean nothing - Social Security number, references, previous employers, addresses, nothing. There's nothing on that application to give a clue of who he is and what he's doing here." They both were mystified.

They were leaving the factory a few minutes after four. Jessie Wayne almost pulled out in front of a passing car when he saw the two-tone pick-up parked across the street from the plant entrance. "Good Lord! There he is!" he exclaimed. The bushy haired man sat behind the wheel reading a magazine. The sunglasses were still in place. As they drove by, he gave no indication of paying any attention to them.

He took Lissie Sue on home and lingered a while before heading out to the farm. As he left the outskirts of town, he happened to look in his rear view mirror. His heart jumped up in his throat. About a hundred yards behind him was the two-tone truck. No matter at what speed he drove, the truck maintained about the same distance back. When he got to the lane leading to the farm, he pulled in and stopped and sat looking in his rear view mirror. The truck just drove on by at the same speed. The sun-glassed driver did not even glance his direction.

Jessie Wayne was jumpy all evening. He kept the front porch light on and went to the door several times and looked out. He half expected to see the bushy haired man standing on the porch but all was quiet and normal. Meanwhile, in a cheap motel in Selma the bushy haired man had removed his sunglasses and was practicing his penmanship on a yellow legal pad.

***

As he left for work the next morning, Jessie Wayne stopped before pulling out on the main road and looked in both directions. There were no vehicles in sight. He turned toward town and kept checking his mirror as he drove. He'd only gone a mile or two when all of a sudden the two-tone truck just seemed to materialize behind him. He couldn't believe it. Where could it have come from? It maintained about a hundred-yard distance on into town. When he turned off to go to Lissie Sue's house, the truck continued in the direction of downtown.

On their way to Boonie Mae's, he told Lissie Sue about the man following him home and then back. "That fellow is really making me nervous," he confided.

Lissie Sue patted him on the arm. "Now Honey, there ain't no need to get all skittish. Things are going too well. Everything is working out just like we planned. We'll soon get all of Nelda Mae's titles transferred to you and then in a month or so you can move in. Anyway, this guy has probably just moved in way out in the county or maybe in the next county."

"Maybe," said Jessie Wayne, "but he gives me the creeps."

As they pulled into the café parking lot, the first thing they saw was the cream and maroon truck parked by the front door. "You want to eat over at The Bus Stop?" Jessie Wayne asked.

"No, we don't need to let no bushy haired stranger spook us. We need to do like we're used to doing." In spite of her words, Lissie Sue's voice had just a little quiver in it.

"Well, okay. But I'm gonna get his license plate number and have Jack Dell run it. I'm gonna find out who this guy is." He jotted it down on a scrap of paper.

They went in and sat in their usual place. The man was at the same table over in the corner, reading a paper and sipping coffee. The sun-glassed eyes were always in view. Jessie Wayne got so nervous that he sat his cup down on the side of his plate and spilled coffee all over the table. The stranger left first. He walked by their booth without even glancing at them. "See," said Lissie Sue, "he don't even know we're in the world." Jessie Wayne was not convinced.

As soon as he got to work, Jessie Wayne got on the phone to the sheriff. He identified himself and asked, "Jack Dell, there's a bushy haired stranger who's been around town for a couple of days. He's driving a two-tone pick-up. Have you seen him?"

"Well, yes, I have as a matter-of-fact. What about him?"

"I'm gonna give you his plate number and I want you to run it. I wanna know who this guy is. And I wanna know what he's been doing around town."

"Is he breaking some law or doing something wrong?"

"Well, not that I know of - but we can't be too careful with them freedom riders coming through all the time. You just check on this. I'll call you back at noon to see what you find out."

"Okay, I'll see what I can do," said Jack Dell as he hung up the phone.

The morning dragged by for Jessie Wayne. But it finally came time for the call. "What did you find out?" he asked as soon as Jack Dell answered the phone.

"Not too much. The truck is registered to a big car dealer in Birmingham. And he's spending most of his time going through country records down in the basement of the courthouse - you know, deeds, titles, births, deaths, marriages and things like that. He's probably just some guy looking for his ancestors."

"I sorta doubt that," said Jessie Wayne, "but thanks anyway." He hung up the phone not knowing much more than before he started.

When they left work that afternoon, they were relieved not to see the two-tone truck parked across the street. "He's probably long gone," said Lissie Sue.

"I hope you're right. But I still don't feel easy." Jessie Wayne was still jumpy.

He didn't linger at Lissie Sue's that day. Said he had to get on home - but he didn't go straight there. He drove all over town looking for the stranger's truck. It was nowhere in sight. He started out the road to the farm but at the edge of town, he pulled behind a vacant building where he could see the road and waited. Two or three vehicles passed but no two-tone truck. Maybe Lissie Sue was right. Maybe the stranger had gone and he'd just gotten worked up over nothing. Finally, he pulled out and headed for home. No truck in sight. After a mile or two, he began to breathe easier. But a glance in the mirror almost caused him to run off the road. There was the truck behind him at the usual distance. In a panic, he pressed the accelerator to the floor and began to drive at breakneck speeds. The truck did not try to keep up and soon faded from view. He threw up a shower of gravel as he turned into the farm lane and raced back to the house. He parked at the front gate, cut the engine, and sat back exhausted. For some reason, he felt safe. Then, he heard another vehicle and looked up as the cream and maroon truck rolled to a stop beside him.

This was all that he was gonna take. He jumped out and ran around to the driver's side of his visitor's truck. The stranger had gotten out and was taking the black rucksack out. "Just who in the hell are you and just what in the hell do you…" He stopped in mid-sentence. The stranger slid his hand into the bag and pulled out a large pistol.

For the first time the stranger spoke. "Time for you to shut up and listen. I'd just as soon kill you as look at you so just do exactly what I say."

"I ain't got no money," Jessie Wayne whined.

"Maybe you're hard of hearing. I told you to shut up. About two more words and you're a dead man. Now, turn around and walk." Jessie Wayne was shaking all over. The stranger walked him around the house to the back yard gate. "Open it. There's a path there. I think you know where it goes." They got to the barn door. "Open it. Go on to the tack room." They stopped in front of the locked door. "Open it."

"I ain't got no key," Jessie Wayne's voice was barely audible.

Suddenly, the stranger rammed the barrel of the pistol into the back of Jessie Wayne's head. "Then you'd better find one quick 'cause if you don't, your brains are gonna be all over this barn." Jessie Wayne reached up and got the key and after several tries managed to unlock the lock.

They went in. Jessie Wayne turned his face away from the letters in the cotton basket in vain hope that they wouldn't be noticed. But the stranger called attention to them by kicking the basket with the side of his foot and saying, "Looks like there's enough violations of the U.S. Postal Laws in here to send you to a federal pen for a long time."

Jessie Wayne did not respond because he did not know what to say. His captor continued, "But that's the least of your worries right now. Open the medicine cabinet." He did. "Now hand it to me."

"Ain't nothing here but some old horse medicine," croaked Jessie Wayne.

Again the pistol rammed the back of his head. "I'm about to lose patience with you. Quit playing dumb. I said get it." The sound of the pistol being cocked spurred Jessie Wayne to action. He knocked down a couple of bottles before he drew down the container of arsenic. "Don't turn around. Hand it back over your shoulder." The stranger took it and placed it in the rucksack. From the bag he pulled out a set of handcuffs. "Put your hands behind you," he ordered. He cuffed Jessie Wayne's hands. "That'll keep you from getting any stupid ideas. Now, let's go in the house."

As they walked back to the house, Jessie Wayne's mind began to work a little. This stranger seemed to know where everything was and something about him was vaguely familiar. When they got into the house, it suddenly dawned on him. "You're Randall Lee," he said. There was relief in his voice. "I sure am glad it's you."

"No, you're not," snarled Randall Lee. "You'd be better off seeing the devil himself right now than me. Now sit." He pointed to a ladder-back chair that faced away from the sink and kitchen counter. "And put your arm behind the back as you sit down." He did so. For the first time Randall Lee took off his sun glasses and put them in the bag. From it he drew out several pieces of rope. He took one piece and tied it around Jessie Wayne's chest and chair back. Each leg was tied to a front chair leg just above the ankle. Then he took the handcuff off his right wrist and hooked it around one of the chair rungs, leaving his left arm tied down and only his right free. From the black sack he took out a pair of surgical gloves and put them on. He intended to leave no evidence that he'd ever been in the house.

"What are you going to do?" asked Jessie Wayne. His voice was shaky and weak.

"It's not so much what I'm gonna do as it is what you're gonna do. You see, you sorry bastard, you killed my mama. But you've been feeling real bad about it and you just can't live with yourself anymore so you've just decided to end it all and kill yourself." He took a folder out of the bag and slipped a sheet of paper out of it.

"It's all right here written on stationery from Lissie Sue's office. I think I've got your handwriting and signature down pretty good."

Jessie Wayne had begun to cry. Tears and slobber ran off his chin. "It was Lissie Sue's idea," he sobbed. "I wouldn't a'done it if it hadn't been for her."

"I'm not surprised. But you did the deed. You bought the poison. You put it in her food and you went off and left her to die like a dog. Of course, I've got some plans for Lissie Sue as well. You even implicate her in your suicide note."

"Please don't kill me," begged Jessie Wayne. "I'll sign the farm over to you."

"This is not about the farm. You can't just give me what I'll get anyway. I've been in the county records. You have no direct heirs. Both yours and Mama's names are on the deed and I'm the closest heir. You can't give me what's really mine and what I'm gonna get anyway."

"The sheriff will have you in jail," Jessie Wayne was grasping at straws.

"You know as well as I do that Jack Dell Lipsey couldn't find his ass with both hands in broad daylight. Anyway, he knows I went back to Denver ten days ago. And this is a suicide. He wouldn't even know how to look at it as a murder."

"Please, please, please don't do it," Jessie Wayne was crying harder and he had lost control of his sphincter muscle and urine was running down his legs and down the front of the chair. "I'll do anything. I'll leave the country and you'll never see me again. Just don't kill me."

"Shut up your sniveling. It's time to get down to business. Your note doesn't say how you're going to do it so we have some options. How about this gun? I got it off the street in Birmingham so it can't be traced. One shot to the temple would do it but that's too quick. I think you're feeling so remorseful that you want to go the same way my mama did with the arsenic."

"No, no, not that. Just shoot me." Jessie Wayne slumped in the chair. His drool wet the front of his shirt.

Randall Lee's voice got angrier. "You know what it's like, don't you, you sorry sack of shit. You watched my mama die. Now it's your turn." Jessie Wayne just moaned and blubbered. "But now you listen carefully. I'm gonna give you a chance you didn't give my mama." Randall Lee picked up the gun and stuck it to Jessie Wayne's right temple. "One little pull on this trigger and you're one-hundred percent dead but I'm gonna give you some hope. I'm gonna mix up two drinks - one with arsenic and one without - and you're gonna get to choose which one you drink. If you pick the one with the poison, you're still dead. But if you get the clean one, you get to live. But you'll sign the farm over to me and you'll take Lissie Sue and leave for parts unknown and if you ever show your face around here again, you're as good as dead. Don't you think that's a pretty good deal? Sure dead for a fifty-fifty chance?"

Jessie Wayne bobbed his head up and down and grunted his ascent. Randall Lee had learned in Korea just how strong hope was. As long as a man has a little hope, he'll try to struggle through most anything, grab at any straw.

Randall Lee went over to the cabinet, which held the liquor and opened it. "Do you like your arsenic with scotch or bourbon?" he asked. There was not an immediate response. "Come on, make a choice. I don't have all night."

"Scotch," croaked Jessie Wayne.

"Scotch it is then." Randall Lee got the bottle out and selected two glasses from another cabinet. He got the poison from his bag. Jessie Wayne could hear the pouring and the stirring with a spoon. "How about a little ice?"

"Okay."

Randall Lee went to the refrigerator and got four cubes for each glass. He sat them on the table where Jessie Wayne could reach them. "I put them in amber glasses so you can't see any particles."

Jessie Wayne sat starring at the glasses with a blank look on his face. He made no move to pick up either one. "Go ahead," commanded Randall Lee. "Waiting's not going to change anything." Jessie Wayne still did not move. "Well, I guess we'll just have to go with one hundred percent then," he said as he picked up the pistol and cocked it.

"No, no. I'll pick one," said Jessie Wayne. He wiped his hand off on his pant leg and stretched it out toward the glasses. He ran his fingers down the sides, feeling the already condensing moisture from the heavy air. He looked at Randall Lee, searching for any clue as to which was the deadly potion. There was none. He finally selected the one on the left.

Randall Lee moved the other glass back to the counter by the sink. "Now drink," he ordered. "And you better not spill it. If you do, it's a bullet." Jessie Wayne drank. It took him three or four minutes to get the six ounces of liquid down. When he sat the glass down, Randall Lee moved it to the other side of the table out of his reach.

"Did I pick the right one?" he asked.

"I guess that all depends on how you want to look at it. You'll know pretty soon."

They sat for perhaps two minutes without speaking before Jessie Wayne said, "I feel kinda funny."

"It may just be that scotch on an empty stomach," replied Randall Lee.

"Yeah, I bet that's it. I got the right one and you just don't want to tell me. That's it, ain't it?"

Randall Lee did not respond to the question but just sat looking at his victim. It wasn't long before Jessie Wayne said, "I don't feel so good." Randall Lee got up, went to the sink, and poured out the other glass. He washed and dried it and put it back in its place. He came back and sat down before speaking.

"It really didn't make any difference which one you picked. I put poison in both of them."

Jessie Wayne's scream could have been heard a long way off had there been anyone to hear him. By this time his body was beginning to twitch and convulse. "You lied to me! Damn you! You lied to me!" He began to retch.

"Do you think you'll ever be able to forgive me?" asked Randall Lee sarcastically.

By this time Jessie Wayne's body was jerking out of control. The violent spasms caused the chair to turn over. The room was filled with his moans, half-screams, and crying with his body jerking against the restraints. Randall Lee sat and watched dispassionately as his mother's killer died.

When all the movement and sound had ceased, Randall Lee got up and felt for a pulse below his ear. There was none. He opened the rucksack and took out a trash bag. He took off the ropes and handcuffs and put them in the bag and put it back in the rucksack. The pistol went in as well. He moved the used glass back to Jessie Wayne's side of the table. The suicide note was placed in the center of the table with the wiped down arsenic container on it like a paperweight. The bottle of scotch went on the table as well. There was an hour or so of daylight left but he turned on the kitchen light. He looked around carefully. It was a good-looking suicide scene. He went out the front door, leaving it unlocked.

Only then did he remove the gloves and put them in the rucksack.

***

Lynn Larson was working late in his office when the phone rang. A disguised voice said, "There's a big story out at the Lattimore place. The doors are unlocked. Don't forget the barn." The line went dead. He grabbed his camera and note pad and practically ran to his car. As he sped through town, he met the two-tone pick-up he'd been seeing around town. The sun glassed driver waved to him. "That's strange," he thought. The truck continued on through town to the main highway and turned toward Birmingham.

***

It was a few minutes past ten that night and Lissie Sue Haycraft sat in a rocking chair on her front porch, sipping on a beer. She was trying to cool off before she went to bed. She wore only a shortie nightgown but no one could see her from the street. The two large oak trees cut off the streetlight's beam and cast a heavy shadow over the porch. Everything was quiet, which magnified the sound of approaching car engines. She was surprised when a patrol car and another car stopped in front of her house. She recognized Sheriff Jack Dell Lipsey as he got out with a deputy. She also recognized the following car's occupant as Lynn Larson, the owner of the local paper. He carried a camera in one hand. They all started up toward her house. She turned up the bottle and drained the last of the beer.

She thought to herself, "Wonder what they could be wanting with me?"

The Undertaker

Spring had come to the mountains of east Tennessee. Laban Snoddy stood in the front doorway of his funeral home and watched the mid-morning sun light up the two rows of yellow jonquils on each side of the walk that led through the maze of blank tombstones down to the street.

From his vantage point, Laban could see most of the town and the valley beyond until it made an abrupt turn around the next mountain--all his domain. His because he was the only undertaker and his was the only funeral home for miles around. None of the other mountain villages had one. The closest one was thirty-eight miles away in Greeneville. If anyone in the area had a directed funeral, it had to be done by Laban's Eternal Rest Funeral Home. Yes, Laban's domain was vast.

The sunlight passed through the old stained-glass panels that formed a border to the beveled glass of the upper half of the door and threw a multicolored pattern on the hardwood floor around Laban's feet. Life was good--but it had not always been so.

Laban had grown up in one of the hollows near town. His parents were poor--as were most inhabitants of the region. But, Laban did not mind the poverty as much as he minded his name. He hated the name Snoddy and the cruel comments his schoolmates made about it. They regularly changed it to "Snotty" and made all sorts of jokes about that nose discharge.

He wanted to quit school, but his mama wouldn't hear of it. Even when he got big enough to be of help to his father around their hillside farm, his mama was unmovable. "My boy's gonna have a ed-jew-ka-shun," she would say, accenting each syllable equally.

Neither she nor her husband had any. With only two or three years of schooling, they were barely literate. Education to her meant finishing high school, and Laban eventually resigned himself to it. To escape some of the torment, Laban retreated into his books and became the "smart boy" in the class.

Anyway, high school was not as hard as grammar school had been. Most of his major tormentors had dropped out by the end of the eighth grade. Some a year or two earlier than that if they'd been held back any. Laban had already had the satisfaction of burying some of them--victims of the roadhouse brawls, jealous husbands, reckless driving, and lawmen's bullets--and he looked forward to providing his services to others as the need arose.

It was during high school that Laban had begun to work for Jubal Pickett, the local undertaker. Even though jobs were few, most boys his age would not even consider such work. "I ain't gonna fool around with no dead folks," was the response he heard from most of his peers. But Laban didn't mind. He told his detractors that dead people didn't bother him nearly as much as the live ones did. Anyway, the job helped his folks out and put some money in his pocket as well.

When it really came down to it though, Jubal wasn't much of an undertaker. He rented a little two-room concrete-block building on the edge of town. The front room was furnished with five or six caskets sitting up on saw horses and an old wooden desk from which business was conducted. The back room held the embalming table and the instruments necessary to perform that function. There was also the "lay-out" table on which the body was dressed and made ready before it was placed in the casket.

Laban was fascinated with all this but, more importantly, he soon came to recognize the possibilities of a good undertaking business. What's more, Jubal was getting old, and with no family it would be easy for someone either to acquire or to buy the business. Laban set about getting himself in position to be that person.

He had only been employed about six months when he found an ad in one of Jubal's trade magazines offering an embalming course by correspondence if you worked with a licensed embalmer while taking it. Jubal was willing to help Laban, and, in fact, had taught him most of the basic procedures already. Anyway, the ad promised a complete refund if the student did not pass the state exam on the first try.

Figuring he couldn't lose, Laban depleted his bank account and sent off his application to the Midwest School of Embalming and Taxidermy making sure to check the correct box. Neither the course nor the state exam was very difficult and Laban became a licensed embalmer during his junior year in high school. He framed both his license and the embalming school diploma and proudly displayed them on the wall behind the cluttered desk.

Laban knew he would need much more money for the next step, so he became more miserly. By the time he graduated from high school, he had saved enough to attend the McDowell School for Mortuary Science in Bristol. But he did not commit himself to that before he got Jubal to agree to sell him the business when he got ready to quit. Jubal was getting tired and was happy to see that there was someone who actually wanted to continue his undertaking parlor. He also knew that Laban would do most of the work once he got his mortician's license. So he even offered Laban a small amount of financial help while he was in school.

Before long, two more frames were added to the wall behind

the desk and Laban began to wear a long-sleeved white shirt and tie to work as symbols of his more elevated status. And much to Jubal's delight he made some changes that increased business. Yes, Laban Snoddy was definitely a young man on his way up.

Within two years, Jubal's health began to decline at a rapid pace. A lifetime of moonshine, tobacco, and the inhalation of embalming fluid fumes all seemed to catch up with him at once. When he realized that the decline was permanent, he offered to fulfill his agreement and sell out to Laban.

But Laban had no intention of remaining in the little concrete block building. He wanted a "real" funeral home--one with a chapel for funeral services, family viewing parlors, display rooms, and all the other things necessary for a modern funeral home.

Laban made an appointment with the president of the local bank, put on his best funeral suit, and made his pitch. He proposed to buy Jubal's business and an appropriate location at the same time. He'd long had his eye on the old, rambling Railroad Hotel located in the center of town a block from the railroad station. With the decline of rail travel, the hotel had fallen on hard times and it was common knowledge that it could be had for a very good price.

The banker liked Laban's proposal and recognized his business sense. He agreed to finance the project, so Laban bought the hotel and all the furnishings. He especially wanted the furnishings because they were all original, dating back to the 1880s. He was sure they would fetch a good price on the antique market, and he was right. The things which could be used in the funeral home were kept. The rest were sold to select dealers and brought almost enough to cover the remodeling expenses. Yes,

Laban did have a good feel for business.

The business prospered receiving an added boost during its third year with the addition of a line of tombstones. Laban managed to secure a local franchise from a monument company in Kingsport. The front lawn which sloped naturally down to the street made an excellent display area. That same year, Laban added the sale of burial policies to his endeavors. The Eternal Rest Funeral Home was one of the few growing businesses in town and Laban Snoddy was its driving force.

The rising sun struck a section of the stained glass at a new angle sending a bright beam of gold light directly into Laban's eyes. Turning away from the glare, Laban saw Peck Henson coming up the drive. Peck was his handyman, doing everything around the place from custodial work to minor repairs to helping with funerals. Peck was OK, but he was not nearly as good as Stimpy, his first handyman. Laban didn't think he'd ever forgive Sam for what he did to Stimpy.

Sam Bannan was not a native. He was from somewhere in the flatlands. He had started to mortician's school but had dropped out from lack of funds and was working to save up enough to finish. Laban had hired him as his assistant when he discovered that he was having a problem getting everything done with part-time help.

Sam loved to joke around--not unlike many undertakers Laban had come to know. You see, most undertakers are not caught up in emotions of the moment. Friends and relatives may cry about the demise of Aunt Hattie, but she's just another body to most undertakers. And although they may present a somber front to the family, behind the scenes they're probably laughing. Sam was like this, but too much so. On more than one occasion,

Laban had had to quiet him down.

Sam even went to a meeting in Knoxville and saw a hearse with a special license place that read, "STIFONE." Immediately upon his return, he wanted to get a special plate for Laban's new hearse that read, "DED 'N GON," but Laban wouldn't hear of it. It was a good thing, too, because a couple of months later a big story hit the newspaper about the Knoxville plate. It seems a bereaved family was following the hearse to the cemetery when they realized what the plate said. They stopped the procession on Kingston Pike in the middle of rush hour traffic and refused to have their loved one transported any further in a vehicle that had "STIFONE" on the back. The undertaker called for a spare hearse which was rushed right out. The only trouble was it said "STIFTWO," and the family wouldn't have it either. He finally borrowed a hearse from another funeral home, but not before the police issued him several citations for obstructing traffic.

The family also filed a lawsuit for the extreme mental anguish they suffered. Laban just looked at Sam and said, "I told you so." But that didn't slow Sam down much.

Stimpy Bledsoe was sort of the town drifter. He was limited both mentally and physically. People said all his problems were caused by a careless midwife at his birthing. A lack of oxygen had caused some brain damage and his left leg got all twisted up so that it did not grow properly ending up about three inches shorter than the right and giving him a rather peculiar gait. He was also very short. Maybe a couple of inches under five feet. Laban guessed that his limping and shortness had somehow been combined into "Stimpy." No one knew his real name--or if he even had one.

Stimpy had spent most of his life doing odd jobs around town.

He worked hard and was reliable but there was a limit to the things he could do. Laban felt sorry for him and gave him his first real job as his handyman and Stimpy turned out to be good at it. The one drawback was Stimpy's superstitious fear of dead people. Laban helped him overcome some of it, but Stimpy was hard to teach and slow to learn, and it was this fear and Sam Bannan that caused Laban to lose Stimpy's services.

It all started innocently enough. Sam took one of the hearses down to the garage to be serviced. While there, he got to talking and swapping stories with some of the town loafers. One thing led to another and Sam decided to play a joke on Stimpy. He put one of the men in the back on the rolling stretcher, pulled a sheet over him, and drove back to the funeral home. He backed the hearse up to the side door where they unloaded the bodies and called for Stimpy to come help him get the "body" inside. Stimpy came with much reluctance and took one side of the stretcher. As they rolled it to the rear of the hearse, the "body's" arm fell off and flopped onto the floor. Sam looked across and said, "This one's so fresh he's not stiff yet. Stick that arm back under there." Stimpy gingerly took the cuff of the shirt between his thumb and forefinger and poked the loose arm back under the sheet.

When they set the stretcher down on the ground, the arm fell out again. Sam, sounding annoyed, said, "Stimpy, put that arm under there good or we're going to end up breaking it and then there'll be hell to pay."

Stimpy dutifully bent down to attend to the arm again when it came alive. The hand ran up his leg and grabbed him in the crotch. Stimpy shot straight up in the air about four feet like he'd been shot out of a catapult and let out a scream that was heard all over town. On the way his legs began to pump like a sprinter and his feet became a blur. Somehow he managed to turn 180 degrees while in the air and land with his back to the "body." His feet were going so fast when he hit the driveway that several layers of rubber from his Converse tennis shoes (Chuck Taylor model) became skid marks on the concrete before he got enough traction to propel himself away from the hearse and toward the street emitting that God-awful scream every few steps.

Sam was amazed. For someone who could not walk very well, Stimpy ran like a world class runner. He took the shortest route to the street which was through the maze of tombstones jumping over the taller ones with a hurdler's form reminiscent of Jesse Owen in the 1936 Olympics. He was gone from sight in just a few seconds but the screams continued to be audible for several minutes.

When Stimpy did not come back to work for several days, Laban went looking for him. He finally found him but there was no getting him to come back. Sam's joking had run off a perfectly good handyman. That was almost two years ago and Laban still couldn't forgive him.

Stimpy's departure had led to the hiring of Peck Henson. Peck wasn't bad--but he was slow. Laban had not been able to find a way to get him to work at even an average pace much less at a fast one. However, to his credit Peck would stay on after quitting time when necessary, without complaining, to get his assignments done. That was a plus. Another plus was the fact that he was not afraid of dead folks. Sam said that he was too lazy to be scared, that being scared took up more energy than he was willing to use. Anyway, he was good help with the bodies.

As far as Laban was concerned, the most frustrating thing about Peck was his disappearing act. He hadn't been working long when Laban notice that Peck seemed to disappear for long periods of time. There seemed to be no pattern insofar as to when he disappeared. It could be at any time. The only thing predictable was the certainty of his disappearance--once a day for an hour to an hour and a half.

Laban at first thought Peck was slipping down the back alley to Wendall's One Stop. Wendall sold beer openly and other assorted spirits from under the back counter. But Laban could never find Peck down there. After questioning all the other owners of nearby businesses and finding no one who'd ever seen Pick during working hours, Laban had to rule out his leaving the funeral home and Peck's "jes bin on break" was not satisfying.

Finding out where Peck was going and what he was doing became almost an obsession of Laban's. One day, during one of these disappearances, Laban spent the better part of an hour searching the entire funeral home, but to no avail.

Even with these extended disappearances, Peck would get his work done, but they continued to eat at Laban. What bothered him the most was that he was being outsmarted by an illiterate hillbilly. That really galled him. Then one day several months later and quite by accident the mystery was solved.

Grady Pell had died. The family was not rich, but they had some money and Laban was trying to sell Mrs. Pell one of his higher priced services. She was in the process of selecting a casket and Laban was steering her through the upstairs display rooms. Walking up to his most expensive model, Laban said in his best funeral voice, "This is really a nice one, Mrs. Pell. It even has an innerspring mattress and just look at the quality of the lining." With that he raised the lid keeping his eyes on Mrs. Pell to get her reaction. Her reaction caught him totally off guard.

Her eyes widened in horror and her mouth got even wider and let out a scream that almost ruptured his eardrums. She turned and ran out of the room knocking over a display of burial clothes as she went. Turning to see what had triggered this reaction, Laban saw Peck rubbing his eyes and looking confused from being awakened so abruptly from his afternoon nap.

It took a considerable amount of talking to get Mrs. Pell not to call in a new funeral director. She finally gave in but would not have the innerspring mattress model. Said she just couldn't bear to see Grady put in the ground in a "used" casket.

After the incident, Laban fixed a place upstairs in which Peck could take his "breaks" in exchange for Peck's promise to stay out of the caskets.

A rattletrap car stopped in front of the funeral home. It was so rusty and faded that it was impossible to determine its original color. Some parts were held on by wire and duct tape. The back window was clear plastic taped over the glassless opening. One of the side windows was cardboard cut from a toilet paper box. Laban recognized that the car had to come from some remote hollow way back up in the mountains. And he also figured that its occupants probably looked no better than the car. He'd seen some who had inbred so much in these isolated regions that they practically had no chins, looking as if they were all descendants of Andy Gump.

Two men got out and Laban noted that his assessment of their probable appearance had been correct. One pulled a light blue folder from out of his bib overalls and stood for some time looking back and forth from it to the funeral home sign trying to match the letters to see if they'd come to the right place. Laban recognized the folder as one of his burial policies.

Every time he saw one of his policies in the possession of these kinds of folks, Laban wanted to wring that college kid's neck. He'd been hired one summer to sell burial policies and had done an excellent job. The only trouble was Laban had not intended for him to sell any to these back woods folk. It never occurred to Laban that he would make contact with any of them--but he did and sold several policies before Laban realized what was happening and got him to stop.

These people were not good risks. Many of them died young which caused Laban to lose money when the policies were not close to being paid up.

Satisfied that they were at the right place, the two men started up the walk. Laban went out on the porch to meet them. He did not want them inside with all the mud they had on their boots.

"Could I help you folks?"

Neither answered. The older man with the policy simply thrust it at Laban. Laban took it and flipping is open, noted that it had been issued to Ira Stookesberry.

"Has something happened to Mr. Stookesberry?" Laban asked.

Ever since his bad experience, Laban always tried to find out the cause of death. This bad experience occurred the time he was burying one of these mountain folk who had been killed in a family feud. The other family ambushed the funeral procession on the way to the cemetery. Several were wounded; none were killed, but his new hearse wound up with two bullet holes in the rear door. Laban didn't really care who shot who but he didn't want himself or his hearse to wind up as casualties.

The older man spoke. "Cousin Ira done passed this morning. Jes' fell over inta his grits 'n gravy at breakfast. Broke his coffee cup, too. Weuns didn't know he was even ailing."

Laban breathed a sigh of relief.

"You folks just have a seat here on the porch while I check Mr. Stookesberry's file." Laban went inside and pulled open his burial policy drawer. Ira Stookesberry's premiums were up to date. He wouldn't make any money on this one unless he could sell them some "extras." He went back out on the porch and sat down opposite the two men.

"Everything seems to be in order. Would you folks like to select a better grade of casket for Mr. Stookesberry? Or possibly a vault?"

"Would hit cost anythang?" asked the older man.

"Well, yes. There would be an additional charge depending on the model chosen."

"Ain't that all in th' paper thar? Man what sold hit to Cousin Ira said hit tuk care of everythang."

"Yes. Yes. Everything is included. I just thought you might want something nicer for Cousin Ira."

"Naw. Iffen he didn't have th' buryin' paper, weuns ud jes go down ta th' sawmill an' get some boards an' make 'im a box. Weuns ain't never had no one put inta th' ground inna store bought box."

Even Laban's cheapest funeral was several rungs up the ladder for the Stookesberry family.

"How will I get to Mr. Stookesberry's house?"

"I'll ride wid 'ya. I'll be back as soon as I talk ta th' pitcher-man."

Laban knew that they were going to engage a photographer to come to the house and take a picture of Cousin Ira. They might even have one taken of the whole family around the casket.

Laban knew of some funeral homes that offered such pictures as part of their funeral packages, but he had never done so.

After the two men left, Laban told Sam to get the old hearse ready. Sam hadn't seen the Stookesberrys.

"Why do you want the old one?" he asked. "The new one is ready to go."

"Because I'm probably going to have to go to the backside of nowhere to get this body and I dang sure don't want to tear up the new one."

The older Stookesberry soon returned and he and Laban set out. He didn't say much. Just grunted and pointed at the roads or forks when a change of direction was needed. After they had forded the third stream and the road became only two rutted tracks, Laban began to worry. He had already scraped both sides of the hearse on tree roots and rocks on some of the sharp turns.

When his passenger said with no warning, "Rat cheer," Laban stopped the vehicle. There was no house, only a path that led up the mountain. Upon getting out Laban could just make out a house of some type a hundred yards or so up the mountain. He also could see six or eight men coming down the trail. They had obviously heard the car engine.

They were a rough looking bunch--but polite. Laban got the rolling stretcher out of the back. Two of the men took it and they all headed up the trail. Laban fell in behind, struggling to keep up. The steep incline had him gasping for breath after a few yards. The mountain men climbed it with ease.

The house was nothing to brag about. It clung precariously to the steep face of the mountain looking as if a loud clap of thunder could shake it loose and send it tumbling toward the valley below. It had two main rooms, with a sleeping attic and shed-room kitchen on the rear. A porch ran across the front. From the inside, one could see bits of sky through the warped shingles of the roof.

Laban went inside with the men and made sure that Cousin Ira was strapped down securely. Four men took the stretcher and headed back down the mountain.

***

The older Stookesberry informed Laban that they wanted Cousin Ira's body brought back there and put on the front porch with the lid up. The funeral and burying would be Tuesday at the Full Gospel Tabernacle. That meant two more trips back up the mountain for Laban. Yes, he was going to lose money on the late Mr. Ira Stookesberry.

Except for a few scrapes on the same roots and rocks, the trip down the mountain was uneventful until the last stream was being forded. The right front tire slipped into a deep hole snapping the suspension and steering system. Fortunately, Laban only had to walk about a mile to the main road where he hitched a ride into town. When he thought of the impending towing and repair bills, Laban got angry at Ira Stookesberry for dying so young.

Laban continued to fume about his misfortune with the Stookesberrys, but he and Sam worked hard to get Ira looking good. A poorly made up corpse would be bad for business even if he were losing money on the funeral. They put Ira in the cheapest casket and strapped him down tight so he wouldn't jostle around so much on the trip back up the mountain.

Laban was not about to take his new hearse to deliver the body. The repair shop loaned him a 4-wheel drive pickup for this purpose. The next day they tied the casket down securely in the truck and Laban headed back to the Stookesberry cabin.

He almost forgot the veil. He seldom used one because in his funeral home and in most of the churches, one was not needed. But he knew that considering the obvious lack of sanitation around the Stookesberry place, an open casket on the front porch would be an invitation to every fly in that part of the mountains. Laban couldn't stand to see flies crawling around the face of a corpse. And, besides that, the fly specks always looked bad and were hard to remove.

The trip went much better in the pickup. Several men came down to the road, carried the casket up the mountain and placed it on two sawhorses in the center of the porch. Laban opened the lid, made some final adjustments on Cousin Ira, and put the veil in place.

By this time, everyone was crowding around to have a look at their dead relative, the first in the family to lie in a store-bought coffin. They all were pleased with his appearance. One elderly woman swore that he "looks so natchurl, like he's jes about ta' speak." Laban's chest swelled with pride. He did do good work- -even if he were not happy with the situation.

On Tuesday, Laban took the pickup back up the now familiar roads to pick up Ira Stookesberry, take him to the church, and put him in the ground. On the way his mind turned to just how much money he was going to lose on this one funeral and got mad at the college boy and Ira Stookesberry all over again.

He huffed and puffed up the mountain to get the casket closed up and to supervise its move to his truck. As he got to the porch he noticed that the veil was crooked, but thought little of it. People always raised them to get a better view of the deceased.

But when he got to the casket, he realized that the skewed veil was only a portent of the disarray inside.

Cousin Ira looked nothing like he did when Laban left him. What hair was not sticking up in all directions was down over his face. One arm was mostly down under the body; the other was bent at the elbow with the hand laying over against the coffin's side and the fingers looking like eagle's talons. His shirt was pulled to one side and wrinkled. The collar was turned up with the points framing Ira's now open mouth. The makeup was all smeared and one eye was about half open. One cheek had dirty smudge.

This was the last straw! In addition to the money he was losing, Laban now was going to have to spend a lot of extra time to try to get Cousin Ira to look halfway decent. Why did he have to be cursed with these people? Why could he not get away from their trifling ways? Laban looked around the circle of vacant, placid faces and exploded, "What in God's name have you done to him?"

The elder Stookesberry stepped forward with a look of hurt and surprise on his face. "Why Mister Snoddy, youns done made 'im look sa' good that when th' pitcher-man come, weuns jes' got 'im out, stood 'im up amongst us, an' had a family portrait took."

The Interview

He was getting his desk ready for the interview - no messy piles of paper, all objects in good and balanced order, the photo of his family on the corner at just the right angle. He positioned the interview chair directly in front of the desk and centered the oversized, brass nameplate whose shiny letters against a burnished background read, "Dr. Harvey Tutwyler." He stood behind the interview chair and admired his set-up. The prospect's attention would be focused on the name plate, then on to him as he sat in his large, executive chair and finally to the wall behind his head which was covered with his diplomas and other certificates and awards. His secretary tapped on his door before poking her head in and announcing, "Dr. Tutwyler, your ten o'clock interview is here." He looked at his watch. She was ten minutes early, a good sign. "Please show her in," he said.

A tall, striking young woman was ushered in and offered the interview chair. After the exchange of a few pleasantries, he opened her file folder, the only piece of work on his desk. "As you know, Miss Bradshaw, we are looking to fill an advanced math teaching position. These positions are very hard to fill. You think you can teach at that level?"

"Of course, I do. You've got my file there. I think my resume` speaks for itself."

"Well let's look and see," he said as he began to shuffle through her folder. "I see you were valedictorian in a high school class of 417 and a National Merit Scholar."

"That's correct."

"And you went to Georgia Tech and majored in math. Why

math? Isn't that kind of an unusual field for a woman?"

"I don't think so. I've always enjoyed math and I don't think math has any gender."

"I suppose you're right. I see you graduated Summa Cum Laude and I don't see anything but As on your transcript."

"Well, I did have one B."

"Oh?"

"Yes, it was in Interpretive Dance. My instructor didn't like the piece I created for the final exam."

"What was the problem with it?"

"Well, I did an interpretation of the ancient Egyptians creating geometry which my teacher said had too many angles and not enough curves."

"Not knowing how to respond, Dr. Tutwyler just said "Umm," before continuing. "Then you spent two years teaching advanced math at an intercity high school in Detroit. How did that come about?"

"I joined the Federal program of putting high achieving graduates in failing schools to help them make up lost ground. I figured if I could teach in a school like that, I could teach anywhere."

"You're probably right. I see you were named the school's outstanding math teacher your second year."

"Yes. That may have been partly because of the volunteer tutorial program I organized with the other math teachers to bring up our lowest performing students."

"Very impressive. By the way I see that you are not married." Tutwyler like to make abrupt shifts in an interview just to see the prospect's reaction.

Miss Bradshaw replied coolly, "No. Just haven't found the

right person yet."

Tutwyler's brow furrowed. "I notice you said 'person' not man. You've not one of 'those' types are you?"

She waited a few seconds before smiling sweetly and replying, "Dr. Tutwyler, I don't really think you're suppose to ask personal questions like this in an interview."

"You're right. I apologize. You're right," Tutwyler responded as he began nervously to shuffle the papers in the file.

"May I ask you a question, Dr. Tutwyler?"

"Why yes, of course."

"I see by your name plate that you have a doctorate. What is your subject area?"

"It's educational, specifically education leadership."

"No," Miss Bradshaw persisted, "I mean your academic area like science, math, English, you know."

"Well, I do have an undergraduate major in general social studies - you know sociology, anthropology, geography, economics, history, government, etc."

"A little bit of everything and not much of anything," Miss Bradshaw thought to herself.

"But after five years of teaching, I knew I wanted to go into educational leadership so all my positions and studies have been in that direction. Now, let's get back to you. I see you spent the last two years at M.I.T. in a master's program in math."

"That's right."

"How far along are you?"

"I will finish my degree at the end of the summer. I just about have my thesis finished. It's taking me a little longer because I've been teaching there each semester as well as doing course work."

"Yes, so I see. Your department head wrote a nice letter

supporting you, says you are their top master's student and that they've offered you a teaching position and a place in their doctoral program. My question is, why do you want to teach in high school?"

Well, after teaching at both levels, I just think I can make more of an impact at the high school level."

"That's certainly admirable," responded Tutwyler as he began shuffling through her file, pretending to look for something he knew he wasn't going to find. "Miss Bradshaw, I don't seem to find copies of your gun license or carry permit."

"Don't bother looking. They're not there. I don't own a gun."

"Well, Miss Bradshaw, I'm sure you got the info sheet on school policies with the application. It's stated very plainly that we expect ALL, and I do mean all, our teachers to have carry permits and to have a hand gun in their possession while on campus or at a school event. That's reflected in our new school motto, 'Everybody's Packing,' which is being translated into Latin for our school crest. We think it's the only sane way to combat this recent rash of school shootings."

"Dr. Tutwyler, I don't like guns. I've never owned a gun. I've never shot a gun and I don't intend to start now. Couldn't I just barricade my classroom door and huddle my kids in a safe corner while all the other armed teachers take out the bad guy."

"Now, Miss Bradshaw, you know that just wouldn't be fair. One of my goals as an educational leader is to make sure that every teacher pulls his or her own weight."

"And you would expect me with a small hand gun to confront some idiot with an AK-47 with 40 bullets in the magazine?"

"We think it's the only way."

"Do you realize that statistics show that even trained law

enforcement officers only hit the person they're shooting at 17% of the time?"

"We think we can improve on that with practice. That's why we have an indoor range next to the gym where you all can use your planning period each day sharpening your skills."

"I'd rather devote my planning time to planning and helping students who need it."

"That's very idealistic," Miss Bradshaw, "but we've got to be practical here."

"Well, I think the most impractical thing is teachers with guns."

Tutwyler sat back in his chair and looked at his interviewee for a long moment before speaking. "Miss Bradshaw, because you are such a strong candidate, I am authorized to offer a compromise. If, and I say if, we offer you a contract you could agree to take training and get certified within one year. We have a local branch of a national organization doing our training at no charge. They even helped build our range. And if you don't want to purchase a personal weapon, they will issue you one with any style holster you choose - ankle, hip, shoulder, or whatever. And they will provide all the ammo you use on the range at no charge. They do not want this to be a financial hardship on our teachers. How does that sound?"

Miss Bradshaw rose to her feet. "It still sounds like I'd be required to carry a gun. I'm sure you have other candidates. When might I expect to hear about my application?"

Tutwyler rose as well. "Within a week or so," he answered as they shook hands across the desk. "Thanks for coming in."

"You're quite welcome," she replied as she made her departure.

He sat for a few minutes deep in thought before buzzing his

secretary. When she came in, he handed her the Bradshaw file. "The usual rejection letter on this one," he directed, "And bring me the stack of other math applicants. We're back to square one.".

The Gates of Hell

"... and the gates of hell shall not prevail...."
--Matthew 16:18

February 1948 at The Winslow School

Coach Buck's whistle called the team to the bleachers at the start of Monday's practice. "Okay, you all settle down," he commanded. The players got quiet. He continued as he referred to his clipboard. "Let's see what we're gonna do this week. We've got Gladeville here Friday night and then we go to Paxton Military Academy on Saturday. We'll go pretty hard today and tomorrow. We need a couple of good scrimmages then we'll work on our shooting, plays, and other stuff toward the end of the week. I want your legs to be fresh for the weekend.

He checked his clipboard as he continued, "You shouldn't have much problem with Gladeville if you play your game. We beat them over at their place last month. Now PMA is another story. We haven't played them since I've been here so I don't know much about them. I've been checking the box scores in the papers every week. Apparently they've got a big ole boy inside that scores a good bit and a couple of guards that usually get into double figures. Seems like they don't win too often away from home but they've got a real good home record for some reason."

Tangle spoke up, "At home they've got the 'Gates of Hell.'" All the newer players turned to look at him wondering what he meant.

"What are you talking about, Tangle?" asked Coach Buck.

"Tradition won't let us tell you, Coach. You'll have to see it for yourself," responded Tangle.

"Well, I don't care what they have just so long as they don't put a lid on our basket," responded Coach Buck.

"Okay, let's get on the floor."

As they lined up for the first drill, Lance asked Tangle what he was talking about. "You'll find out soon enough," Tangle replied sounding very mysterious.

The week went quickly and Friday's game with Gladeville went as Coach Buck had predicted. By halftime it was apparent that the visitors were over matched. However, Winslow only won by 15 since Coach Buck played the subs a good bit the second half. He wanted his starters to be fresh for the unknown the next night at Paxton.

On the bus ride to Paxton, Lance heard Tangle and a couple of older players talking. "Wonder what she'll look like this year?"

"There's no telling but you know she'll be a looker."

"That's for sure. I really liked that red head they had three years ago"

"She was nice. Wonder where they get these girls?"

"From the town I'm sure. I hear they've got 'em standing in line for the job."

Lance's curiosity was aroused but he refrained from asking what they were talking about.

Paxton's gym was unusual, to say the least. It was small and there were no seats on the floor level. They were located in a balcony that ran all the way around the building. The team benches and scorer's table was tucked back under the balcony on one sideline Everything about the building seemed old except the clear glass back boards that were attached to the balcony at each end of the court. Lance hadn't seen many glass backboards. They were too expensive for most high schools. Lance figured that PMA had to have them so that those in the end balconies could see. He was soon to find that they served another purpose as well.

All the Paxton cadets were in blue-grey uniforms. Lance thought they looked rather nice. There was a cluster of them directly behind the goal where Winslow was warming up. They jeered every missed shot, waved their hands back and forth, and made faces. They were a little distracting but Lance figured he'd get used to seeing them through the backboard once the game started.

As they were finishing their warm-ups, the crowd of cadets began cheering and clapping. Tangle remarked to one of the other seniors, "Well, I see they've got a blond this year." Lance followed their gazes and noted a good-looking girl being escorted by four cadets. She wore a filmy, blue dress which accented her blond tresses that cascaded around her shoulders. The entourage made its way around the balcony to Winslow's end. The group that had been heckling the visitors made room and the girl and her escorts settled in just behind Winslow's goal. Lance figured she was the cadet queen for the year or something on that order.

The referee came out on the floor and the horn sounded for the game to begin. Tangle controlled the tip and Doggie brought the ball down. Lance and Tangle set up in their customary low post positions. Paxton was playing a man defense. When Doggie gave Lance's signal, Lance rolled around his man and across the key just inside the circle. Doggie hit him with a perfect pass.

Lance took one more step and went up for the hook shot. The ball went off the glass and into the basket. Winslow had drawn first blood. Paxton came down and promptly threw the ball away. Doggie brought the ball down and again called Lance's number. Lance lost his man again and banked in another hook.

Paxton ran a play but missed the shot. Tangle gathered in the rebound. Doggie gave a different signal this time When Lance got loose and got the ball, Tangle's man came over to cut off the hook shot. Tangle cut to the basket, Lance bounced the ball to him, and he laid it in.

Paxton's offense seemed out of sync. One of the guards took a long shot which missed everything. The ball disappeared under the balcony. They were yet to score.

Doggie brought the ball down and passed it to Tangle who broke straight out. He flipped it to Lance who was again breaking across the key. Lance's man was beginning to catch on and was playing Lance close on the inside and was trying to get in front of him to stop the hook shot. Lance faked the hook and his man went into the air. He then put the ball on the floor, whirled to his right, and laid it in the basket with his left hand. The Paxton coach called a time out.

In the huddle Coach Buck said, "Okay, I think we've got 'em a little confused. Doggie, let's keep on working the inside until they stop us. Watch for the adjustments they're making."

On the subsequent trip down, one of the Paxton forwards got loose and hit a short jump shot. Paxton had gotten on the scoreboard.

Their defense looked the same when Winslow came down. But Lance's defender anticipated his route and when he went up for the hook, came crashing into him hitting him across his head and arm as he tried to block the shot. They went down in a heap on the floor; the ball squirted up into the air. The referee blew his whistle. "That's a foul on number 40," he said, "two shots."

As they were untangling the Paxton player snarled, "You're not gonna shoot that shot on me."

"If that's how you're gonna stop it, you'll be fouled out before halftime," responded Lance.

They lined up for the foul shots. Lance took the ball from the referee and bounced it twice. He looked up to focus on the front of the rim expecting to see the cadets waving and trying to distract him. However, they were all sitting without moving. What he did see though just over the rim was the blue skirt slide up exposing two knees. Then the knees began to part revealing two of the whitest thighs Lance had ever seen. The knees continued their divergent paths until the blonde's red-pantied crotch was in full view.

Lance froze. He was glad he was wearing a tight jock strap. He couldn't bounce the ball or shoot. He had never had a girl invite him to look at her privates. The knees snapped back together. "That's ten seconds, son. You don't have all day to shoot the ball," said the referee. "Ball to the white team." "The Gates of Hell" flashed through Lance's mind.

As he headed back down the court, Lance felt his face grow hot in embarrassment. He hated to think how red it had to be. He stole a glance at the bench and saw Coach Buck motioning for a sub. Tangle trotted by him and asked, "Did she open those gates for you?"

"Why didn't you tell me about her?" Lance asked.

"The new have to be initiated," laughed Tangle as he moved away to his defensive position.

When his sub came in, Lance tried to find a seat on the end of the bench away from Coach Buck but it didn't work. Coach called him down to sit beside him. "What the heck happened, son?" he asked. "You were playing like a pro and then you looked like you had an epileptic seizure on that foul shot." Reluctantly, Lance told him what had happened. Coach Buck turned his head and looked up into the balcony. The blond waved to him. "Well, I'll be damned," he said. "And I thought I'd seen about everything."

"But I'm okay, Coach," said Lance eagerly. "Can I go back in?"

"You sure you just don't want another look?" asked Coach Buck half smiling.

"Yes sir, I do. But I'll get my foul shots off."

"Get back on the floor then," directed Coach Buck hardly able to contain his laughter. The word on just what was transpiring spread to all those on the bench. A few began to shout and point at the blond until Coach Buck silenced them.

Lance got fouled again and on his way to the foul line resolved to make the point regardless of the red panties. When he looked up, the knees were already apart and one hand was out front with the index finger crooking as if beckoning to him. Lance's shot ricocheted off the rim and backboard but it came off on Tangle's side who got it and put it in for two points. "Thanks for helping me with my average," joked Tangle as they ran down

"You're quite welcome," responded Lance. "You'd better stay ready. There'll be a lot of chances for put-backs before the game's over." Tangle just laughed.

As it turned out, the blond had any number of other discombobulating moves. Sometimes instead of beckoning she would just point to her crotch; sometimes the hand would be fanning the area as if it were hot; sometimes the knees would just open and shut giving the appearance of a flashing stoplight.

All of this began to effect other aspects of Winslow's game. Coach Buck called a timeout and chewed them out. It didn't do much good. Lance did manage to make a foul shot but it did not go in cleanly. It bounced off the rim and backboard four or five times before it finally fell through. Some of the shots didn't draw iron; Doggie shot one over the backboard and into the balcony.

When the horn sounded to end the first half, Winslow was up 13 points. As they headed for the dressing room, all the starters were dreading facing Coach Buck. Tangle punched Lance in the ribs and said, "I hear that if they're down over ten points at half, she takes off her panties."

"I don't care what she does," responded Lance. "We'll be shooting on the other end." Tangle just smiled knowingly.

Coach Buck took a low-key approach for which everyone was thankful. "I'm sure you all know," he said, "that you should be about 25 ahead right now. You've gotta get your minds off of nookie and into the game." He talked on about concentration and similar things. Lance guessed that Coach thought better of trying to rein in a bunch of horny teenagers who were enjoying the sights they were seeing. Lance was just thankful they'd be shooting on the other goal the second half. Of course, he was not privy to the micro-drama that was being played out upstairs.

After the teams left the court, the blond and her four escorts rose and made their way to the lobby. The cadets clapped and cheered her exit. She headed to the bathroom after giving her order to one of her escorts who went to the concession stand and purchased a large Coke, a large bag of popcorn, and a Milky Way candy bar. Upon her return her retinue buzzed about her like Lords of The Bedchamber around Louis XIV, feeding her

portions of the purchased snacks. After a few minutes, the group
headed back to the arena with one boy carrying the Coke, another
the popcorn. She had eaten the candy bar. Again to the cheers
of the cadet corps, they went to the opposite end of the balcony
where a group of cadets were saving them the strategic seats.
Lance picked up a ball and started to shoot when he saw the blue
dress. His mouth dropped open. She wiggled her fingers at him
in a half wave and smiled revealing the popcorn in her mouth.
"Damn," uttered Lance, "another rough half."

Winslow set up a play on the tip. When the ref tossed the ball
up, Lance broke for the basket. Tangle tipped the ball to Doggie
who hit Lance with a perfect pass. However, one of Paxton's
guards sniffed out the play and caught Lance as he was going in
for the lay-up and fouled him hard. They both went to the floor
and slid up under the balcony. As he got to his feet, he heard the
ref say, "Two shots." "Oh crap," he thought, "here come the red
panties again."

Lance bounced the ball a couple of times with his head down
resolving to ignore the sight he knew he was going to see.
However, he was not prepared for what confronted him when he
looked up and the knees parted. There was no red. What Tangle
had heard was indeed correct. For the first time in his life he was
looking up into a girl's uncovered crotch. His first shot did not
even come close but he made the second. As they trotted down
the court, Tangle asked, "Was I right or not?"

"I'll tell you one thing," responded Lance. "She's a true blond.

When the word got around that the girl was without
underwear, some of the Winslow players were begging the
Paxton boys to foul them. In spite of the distraction, Winslow
continued to pull ahead. As this happened, the girl began to flash

any Winslow player who took a shot in front of the basket. Some went in that area and took poor shots just for the view. This resulted in a time out and a dressing down by Coach Buck.

Early in the fourth quarter, the outcome of the game was no longer in doubt. Coach Buck turned to Coach Brownlee and said, "I guess it wouldn't hurt to let the subs have a look," as he began to send them in.

When the face of the time clock turned red denoting the last minute of play, the blond and her escorts rose and headed to the exit. The cadets cheered her departure. One of her escorts carried her half empty bag of popcorn; she had consumed the coke.

When they got to the dressing room, Coach Buck said "Okay get a shower and get dressed. We'll talk on the bus."

Coach Buck got to his feet as the bus pulled out onto the main highway and stood at the front facing his team. "Okay, let me have your attention for a few minutes." There was immediate quiet. The players were not quite sure what to expect. "Whether you all realize it or not, we have a pretty good basketball team," he continued. "We won easily in spite of some of you going crazy at times. The lesson here is that some teams are going to try to do anything to distract you. And when they do, you've got to keep your head in the game and maintain your concentration. I don't think anybody else will go quite this far but you never know what you're going to run into as we get closer to tournament time. Anyway, a good win. I'll see you at practice Monday."

Everybody was relieved. The ride back was noisy as they kidded each other about who got the best look and speculated on just what acts the blond and her escorts might be engaging in back at Paxton. Lance, for one, appreciated Coach Buck's handling of the matter.

They got back to their rooms a few minutes before lights out. Lane had time to fill Tex in on the events of the evening. Tex was amazed "You mean a good looking girl just let you look at her trim?" asked Tex incredulously.

"That she did, roomie. That she did," responded Lance as they got into bed. The last bell sounded and the lights went out.

"Are there any open slots on the basketball team?" asked Tex.

"Forget it. Something like this will probably never happen again."

"Damn. You round-ballers have all the luck," groused Tex as he rolled over to go to sleep.

A New Pair of Glasses

Charlie Jenkins sat on a bench in the Westtown Mall and bounced his new aluminum cane on the floor between his feet. He got a better bounce than he did at home where Suzy, his wife, fussed about his annoying habit. No one here to fuss and hard carpet over the concrete floor gave a good bounce. When he grew tired of bouncing his cane, he'd take off his glasses and twirl them by one of the ear pieces. He still wore the heavy, dark frames that were in style in the '50s. His friends teased him about looking like a cross between Dave Garraway and Buddy Holly. But his philosophy was "if you find something you like, why change?" The carpet was two or three shades of green with some geometric pattern in the background. He was trying to figure the pattern out but had not yet gotten a handle on it.

His seat was about fifteen feet from the kid's play area which was opposite one of the mall's entrances. He was watching his seven-year-old granddaughter Samantha - Sam for short - while Suzy and their daughter and Sam's mother, Connie, shopped. The mall had just opened and there were not many shoppers. Sam was the only child in the play area. Every so often she'd yell, "Watch this Papa," or "look what I can do," as she came down the slide backward or hung upside down from one of the bars. He watched and commented on her physical prowess.

A young man came walking by. Charlie thought he looked rather odd. He wore jeans, a hooded shirt, dark glasses, and a baseball cap. He had a scruffy beard and the hood was pulled up over the cap so only the bill stuck out. Charlie wondered why the hood was up. It was not cold weather. He slowed his pace as he walked by the play area but continued down the mall.

Charlie banged the cane harder on the floor. He hated to have to use it but he had no choice when the shrapnel in his back acted up as it did more frequently now. He'd gotten it in Korea around the Chosen Reservoir. That seemed so long ago now but the memory was still vivid.

The young man with the hood came back. He stopped and sat down on the two-foot high wall that bounded the play area. For some reason he made Charlie uneasy so he got to his feet to go get Sam. But he was too late. At that instant Sam came sailing down the slide and as she hit the floor, the man's left arm snaked out and scooped her up with one motion. As he headed for the exit, Sam began to scream. The man tried to get his other hand over her mouth but she was twisting and thrashing about so hard that he couldn't. Charlie tried to run knowing he'd never catch the kidnapper. In an act of desperation, he grabbed his cane by the tip and threw it at the fleeing man's legs, hoping he might be able to trip him up. As soon as he turned it loose, he knew he'd thrown it too low and watched as it hit the floor about six feet behind him. But then, the cane appeared to take on new life as it ricocheted off the hard surface and seemed to wind itself around both the man's legs at the same time. As he fell, he released his hold on Sam who went tumbling end over end across the floor. The cane's entanglement threw the man to one side and headlong into a low stone wall around a planter full of shrubs.

Charlie continued his shuffling run toward the man. His mind raced to decide what to do when he got there. He know his 78 year old body would be no match for the younger man but he was going to do something. As he moved across the green carpet, his mind flashed back to the days he played tackle and kicked off for Ole Miss. In those days there were no kicking specialists. Kickers played a regular position and kicked straight on like Lou "the toe" Groza. None of those soccer kickers in his era. You wanted to hit the ball just below the center for slow rotation and greater distance. The collision with the stone had stunned the man and he was just getting up on his hands and knees as Charlie arrive. His shirt was up and his whole side was exposed. Charlie eyed the rib cage just a little below center, planted his left foot, and drove his right toe into the exposed side. He felt ribs crack and heard the man scream. The man rolled over on his back and blood began to come from his mouth. Charlie backed up a few steps. His next target would be his head but Sam thwarted this blow as she came rushing into his arms. He held her tightly as she sobbed uncontrollably.

The next few minutes were a blur. People came from all directions. The man continued to convulse while spitting up blood all over the green carpet. Someone called an ambulance. Mall security officers appeared. Soon Charlie found himself out of the chaos in the mall security office with Sam still clinging to him like a leech. Suzy and Connie came from someplace. Sam finally released her grip around his neck and went to her mother. "What happened, dear?" Connie asked.

"Papa saved me," was all Sam could say.

Charlie told the women what had happened. They sat on a couch together for a long time. Finally, two men came in. "I'm Detective Campbell. This is my partner, Detective Hernandez. We'd like to get your statement while things are fresh on your mind. You think you're up to it?"

"Of course I am," Charlie answered.

Detective Campbell placed a small tape recorder in front or

Charlie and turned it on. Charlie gave him the whole story. "We'll get your granddaughter's statement later after she's settled down some. Your account jibes with the witnesses we've found," Detective Campbell said. "We'll need to keep your cane for evidence."

"That's fine," Charlie replied, "it's bent anyway so I'm gonna have to get a new one." Detective Hernandez left the room, returning in a few minutes with a new walking stick. "Who do I pay?" asked Charlie.

"Nobody," said Detective Hernandez, "compliments of Westtown Mall."

"Now that's real nice of them," said Charlie. "I'll send them a thank-you note."

"I'm sure they'd appreciate it," said Detective Campbell. "Now, I need all of you to do something. We'll get you out a back way to avoid he crowd out front and we'll escort you home. Please do not talk to anyone, make any statements, or give any interviews. The press will probably find you pretty soon so expect a big hub-bub. Can you manage that?"

"I think we can manage that," replied Charlie.

"Good. Here's my card. Call that number if you need me, day or night. I'll be around later today to talk with you after I get some things sorted out. Thank you for your help."

After they got home, Suzy fixed some sandwiches for lunch. Sam was looking forward to eating at the food court but the abductor had messed that all up. Charlie promised her that they'd go back one day soon and just eat. That seemed to satisfy her.

About the middle of the afternoon the doorbell rang. Looking out the front window, Suzy reported, "There's a TV van outside. They've found us." Charlie went to the door and tried to tell the reporter in a nice way that they would not have a statement or give interviews. The reporter was insistent and tried to push the door open, prompting Charlie to shut and lock it A crowd was gathering. Another TV station showed up. They rang the doorbell so much that Charlie disconnected it but that didn't stop their knocking. TV cameras were being held up to the windows so Suzy closed the blinds. They were under siege in their own home. Sam was fascinated with all the commotion. Charlie called Detective Campbell and told him what was happening. "I assume you are requesting that these trespassers be removed from your property," Campbell said.

"You are right about that," Charlie responded.

"We can get them off your property and give you a little breathing room. I'll be right out."

Within a few minutes Detectives Campbell and Hernandez showed up. There was a woman with them as well as a squad car. The uniformed officers began putting up yellow police tape around Charlie's yard. Some loudmouth in the crowd began to shout, "I hope you're here to arrest this criminal for attacking that boy. He ought to be in jail. Put him in jail."

Charlie, Suzy and Connie looked at each other. "There's something about this we don't understand," observed Charlie.

Detective Campbell came up on the front porch and turned to give a statement to the press. "The Jenkins family respectfully requests that you not trespass on their property. So you will need to stay behind the tape. If you do not, you will be arrested. The family has no statement to make at this time and will grant no interviews. Thank you for your cooperation." As the detective came into the house, shouts of "Arrest him," "Put him in jail," came from the loudmouth in the crowd.

"What the hell is going on?" asked Charlie.

"Let's sit down and talk a little," said Campbell. Suzy escorted them all to the back part of the house and seated them around the kitchen table. "First of all, this is Detective Cunningham," said Campbell introducing the woman. "I thought Sam might be more at ease talking to a lady." And looking at Sam who was in Connie's lap, "Honey, do you think you can tell Miss Liz here what you remember about what happened at the mall this morning?"

"Yes, sir," replied Sam.

"Good. Why don't you and your mother go with Miss Liz, maybe back to your room, and you can tell her all about it." As the three got up to leave, he said to Connie. "Your folks can fill you in on what we talk about."

After they'd left the room, Charlie said to Campbell, "There's something funny going on here. All this hoopla. That idiot standing out there calling for my arrest. Just what in the hell's going on?"

"Mr. Jenkins, you are very perceptive," answered Campbell. "That's why I'm here - to get us all on the same page. First of all, does the name J. Patton Vanderpool mean anything to you?"

Charlie's brow furrowed. "You mean THE J. Pat Vanderpool, the construction company that just finished the new convention center, who builds stuff all over this part of the country, the city councilman and Lord knows that else? THAT Vanderpool?"

"Yes. That Vanderpool. Our abductor is his son. Goes by Jason. That'll give you some idea of the hornet's nest you just kicked over this morning."

Charlie's eyes narrowed. "You're not getting ready to ask us to drop the charges are you?"

Before Campbell could answer, Detective Cunningham came back. "We're not through yet but I thought you'd want to know. Sam says she bit his finger when he tried to put his hand over her mouth."

"Good work," responded Campbell as he pulled out his cell phone and dialed a number. When he got his party, he said, "This is Campbell. Jason Vanderpool should have a bite mark on one of his fingers. Get our forensics people to the hospital pronto. I want photos of that mark from every conceivable angle so that we can match it to the teeth that made it." He put his phone away and addressed the Jenkins. "We'll need to take Sam to the dentist tomorrow to get an impression made. I wanna make sure we can match things up. Now, does that answer your question about our sweeping this thing under the rug?"

"Yes, I think so," Suzy answered. "By the way, how bad is he hurt?"

"Well, Mr. Jenkins, you broke three of his ribs and one punctured his lung. That's where all the blood was coming from. The Docs have him patched up. He'll make a full recovery."

"Will he be arrested?" asked Charlie.

"Already has been. We've got a uniform sitting outside his hospital door around the clock until he's well enough to go to jail or be arraigned. That's rankling the hell out of ole J. Pat but I'm trying to piss him off just as much as I can."

"Why do I get the feeling we don't really know the full story?" asked Charlie.

"Because you don't. Let me fill you in because we're going to need a lot of help from you folks to make this case stick. Jason has been molesting little girls for years. Has an extensive juvenile record which is now sealed since he's 22. He's had three arrests as an adult. No trials. No convictions.

"Does he hurt or," Suzy shuddered, "kill these girls?"

"No. At least not yet anyway. He just relies on Daddy's money and influence to get him out of the charges. But he's getting bolder. This is the first time he's tried anything this brazen. We need to get him off the streets before he does kill somebody.

"Why'd he pick Sam?" asked Suzy.

"Just a target of opportunity. One little girl. Few people around. An older man with a cane. He'd probably have taken her off someplace, molested her, and then turned her loose."

Suzy shuttered again just thinking about it. "I should have gone on and stomped the sombitch to death," said Charlie.

"Then you would have a whole bunch of problems. It's best we do this legally."

"Legally hasn't worked too well seems like," Charlie observed. "How's he gotten out of it?

"A combination of money and intimidation. Witnesses clam up and parents refuse to press charges. We know that J. Pat's scared or paid them off but we can't prove it. He's got a lot of influence in this town."

"Well, we're not gonna drop any charges," Charlie promised. "Let's hang his ass this time."

"That's what we want to do but believe it or not it's not gonna be easy. We'll be fighting an uphill battle. Let me tell you why.

> **Number one:** The Police Commissioner and Vanderpool are big buddies. He's pressuring our Chief to make this thing go away. The Chief is not caving in and has promised me full support but he's walking a tightrope.

Number two: We know there are several cops in Vanderpool's pocket. That means I've got to be careful internally with evidence, procedure, etc.

Number three: The mall has two security cameras trained on that play area. For some strange reason, both "malfunctioned" this morning. When we checked we found that they were working perfectly and both were loaded with new tapes. None of the other cameras had new tapes. Vanderpool is a major investor in the mall and was the main force in bringing in this manager two years ago. Go figure.

Number four: We've got three good eye witnesses right now - if they'll hold. Two are store owners in the mall. They'll be under a lot of pressure.

Number five: Vanderpool is trying to paint you as a confused, disoriented old fool who mistakenly attacked his innocent son as he was trying to help your granddaughter. That's the reason for the idiot outside yelling for your arrest. He's getting on TV and clouding the issue."

"That's a lotta bullshit," retorted Charlie.

"Of course it is. But if you pile it up deep enough and put it on the news, somebody is going to believe it. I'm telling you this is not going to be an easy fight. And it's going to be even more difficult because the Chief's determined to take ole J. Pat down with the boy. Things are gonna get rough before this is over. You all need to know that before you sign on. You wanna take a little time to think about it?"

Charlie reached over and took Suzy's hand. They looked at

each other for a few seconds before Charlie spoke. "I don't think we'll need any time. We haven't been in a good fight in quite some time and we may not live long enough to be in another one. And this is something worth fighting for. Sign us up."

"That's great," said Campbell and they shook hands all around.

Detective Cunningham came back with Sam and Connie. "This little lady gave us a great statement," she said, hugging Sam who smiled broadly.

"Are you gonna put that bad man in jail?" asked Sam.

"We sure are, honey," answered Liz.

"Okay, same rules - no statements, no interviews. We'll be back in touch," said Campbell. The officers left but the crowd didn't. The loud mouth idiot was yelling.

For several days none of the family could get out of the driveway or go anyplace without being photographed and having questions shouted at them. But you can only take so many pictures of ordinary folk going to the grocery store, drug store, and dry cleaners and getting no response to your questions before getting discouraged and quitting. Even "loud mouth idiot" quit showing up.

Detective Hernandez came by with disturbing news. "We've only got one witness left," he reported. "The store owners have had memory lapses. We're sure J. Pat has threatened them with eviction and no telling what else but their lips are sealed right now."

"Well, you said this wasn't gonna be easy," responded Charlie.

"No. It's not." agreed Hernandez. "You folks still with us?"

"Of course we are," answered Charlie. "I'm getting more pissed off at Vanderpool every day."

"Good. Do you always wear glasses like that?"

"Sure do. Something wrong with them?"

No. We just think you need a new pair for this case."

"Why would I need a new pair?" asked Charlie. "I like these."

"What I really mean is a new pair that looks like those. You'd be surprised how small microphones and cameras are these days. Do you have another pair we can use as a model?"

"Sure do," answered Charlie. He left the room and soon came back with another pair.

"It'll take a few days to get this done. Then we'll be back in touch," said Hernandez as he took his leave.

A few days later both Campbell and Hernandez came by with the new glasses. "More bad news," reported Campbell. "We now have no witnesses."

"How in hell did that happen?" asked Charlie.

"Well, she's a young, single mom who works in a beauty shop. When I saw her yesterday, she was driving a brand-new BMW and she wasn't real sure what she saw. It doesn't take a rocket scientist to figure out what happened. We're working to see if we can trace the car purchase back to Vanderpool but that's a long shot, considering all his businesses and connections."

"Now I'm really pissed off," said Charlie.

"Welcome to the club," said Campbell. "But that's not gonna hang J. Pat. We've gotta plan but it all hinges on you all and especially you, Mr. Jenkins. Think you're up to it?"

"Bring it on. That bastard needs his ass kicked."

"Okay. You do realize that J. Pat now has you isolated. We have no film and no witnesses. All we have is a bite mark and you and Sam's testimony. If you flake out, we don't have anything."

"We're not about to quit," vowed Charlie.

"Alright," said Campbell, "Let me lay out some things. Jason is going to be well enough for arraignment pretty soon. Vanderpool is going to start putting pressure on you to back out before this happens. He knows that if he can, we don't have a case, so expect some contact from him pretty soon. We don't know who he'll use but he'll be having someone else doing his dirty work. We've gotta get to him some way and tie him to all this witness tampering. How good an actor are you?"

"Well," answered Charlie, "I had a part in a play in high school." Campbell rolled his eyes before he realized Charlie was teasing him. "Seriously, I spent over 40 years in coaching, teaching, dealing with kids and parents. I know how to act."

"Okay," replied Campbell, "here's what we're going to do. We are going to put a tap on your phone. J. Pat will undoubtedly tap it also so be aware of that."

"Are you serious?"

"Dead serious. Make all calls to me on your cell. I'll do the same to you. And we are going to put tracking devices on your cars so we won't spook anybody by having to follow too closely. But we'll be around any meetings you have. You can rest assured on that. Just don't look for us. Somehow we've got to get beyond all the layers Vanderpool uses to deflect his involvement."

"Where do the glasses come in?"

"They come in any time you're talking to or are with anybody from J. Pat's camp. The on/off switch is right here. Just press it. It will be taking pictures of anybody you're looking at and recording your voices at the same time. Speak normally. Vanderpool's bunch are going to be very skiddish about wires. We hope this will fool them."

"Do you think we'll be in any danger?" asked Suzy.

"We don't think so," answered Campbell. "Vanderpool has never done anything violent but that's why we're taking all these precautions. And one thing be sure of, don't ever meet with them anywhere except a public place. There's more safety in a lot of people."

"What do we do next?" asked Charlie.

"Just wait," said Detective Hernandez. "If he's gonna make a move, he'll make it soon. We'll have some people come out this afternoon and put the trackers on your vehicles. They'll be in a TV repair truck. Don't forget that Vanderpool will have you under surveillance as will we. So don't do anything at anytime that might give things away."

"We won't but just knowing that gives me the willies," said Charlie.

After the detectives left, Charlie, Suzy, and Connie just sat looking at each other for a time. "Makes me wonder just what I've gotten us into," said Charlie.

Suzy hugged him. "We're all in this together, honey," she said. "You know we're doing the right thing."

"I hope it turns out that way," replied Charlie.

They didn't have long to wait. Two days later a call came in. The male voice said, "I'm trying to reach Mr. Charlie A. Jenkins."

"You've reached him. What can I do for you?"

"You don't know me, Mr. Jenkins. My name is Lester Fitzhugh. I'm an attorney. Do you have any relatives in Arizona around the Flagstaff area?"

"Well, yes. But I've lost contact with them."

"Well, I've been contacted by an executor of an estate out there looking for heirs. You might have come into a share of an inheritance."

"This is not one of those Nigerian scams, is it?"

"No. No. Nothing like that. This won 't cost you anything."

"Who died?"

"We just need to meet so I can fill you in on everything and verify some stuff."

"Do I need to come to your office?"

"No. Why don't we meet over lunch. I'm open today if you are. That will save me some time. I'll buy."

"Sure. When and where?"

"Let's meet at ll:30 at The Roundtree. Will that work for you?"

"It will. I'll see you there."

As Charlie hung up, he said to Suzy, "They've made contact."

"What did they say?" she asked.

"It's more what they didn't say. They've done their homework. I had an uncle who went out west a number of years ago to seek his fortune. He never found it. The last we heard from him he didn't have a pot to piss in or a window to throw it out of. I'm sure there's no estate but it's a good play. And this "lawyer" who's meeting me for lunch didn't bother to set up some way for us to recognize each other. I'm going to go early and just sit in the foyer and see if he picks me out. I'll bet he knows what I look like."

"This is beginning to sound a little scary," said Suzy. "You will be careful, won't you?"

"Of course, I will, dear. I'll call Campbell before I go."

Charlie sat waiting with several others at the restaurant, staring at nothing in particular. A large man in a blue pin-stripe suit and bow tie, carrying a brief case, came in and made a bee-line for him. Charlie adjusted his glasses and waited. The man stopped in front of him. "Are you Mr. Jenkins," he asked. Charlie nodded. The man stuck out his hand. "Lester Fitzhugh. We can go on in. I've called for reservations."

They were seated and exchanged comments about the weather. They both ordered sandwiches. Then, Charlie brought up the estate thing. "What's this about an inheritance? My Uncle Albert died several years ago."

Fitzhugh leaned forward. "Well, you see, this really isn't about an inheritance. It's about a legal matter you're involved in."

"And just what legal matter would that be?"

"The one involving that innocent young man you so brutally attacked without provocation."

Charlie's eyes narrowed. "You know as well as I do that's a bunch of horse shit."

"Well, Mr. Jenkins, I'm not here to argue that point at the moment. I'm here representing a party who would like to effect a mutually beneficial resolution to the issue."

"And just who might this party be?"

"I'm not at liberty to say at this point."

"Then I won't be able to talk at this point." Charlie's voice was firm. "I don't know you from Adam's off ox. I don't know who you supposedly represent. I'm not about to talk to some errand boy from God knows who. I need to talk to the source directly or you've just made a poor lunch investment." Charlie hoped he hadn't gone too far but there was no turning back now.

"Surely, Mr. Jenkins, you can figure out . . . "

Charlie cut him off. "I'm not in the figuring out mode. I want to speak to the top dog or we have nothing left to say."

Fitzhugh sat looking at Charlie for a long moment.

"Would a phone call suffice?"

"It would be a good start."

After another long look, Fitzhugh asked abruptly, "Are you wearing a wire?"

"A what?" Charlie played dumb.

"A wire, a microphone, a recorder."

"Hell no. Why would I be doing that?"

"Then you wouldn't mind if I checked before we go any further."

"Of course not."

Fitzhugh took a canvas bag out of his case and motioned for Charlie to follow him to the bathroom. He led him into the handicapped stall. "Put everything from your pockets into this bag," he directed. Charlie did so. "Open your shirt." He ran his hands all over Charlie's torso, front and back. He examined Charlie's belt. "Put your belt in the bag." He then gave Charlie's lower body a thorough pat down. "You're clean," he declared.

"Told you so," said Charlie as he got his clothes back in order. When they got back to their table, their sandwiches had arrived. Fitzhugh put the bag into his briefcase and snapped it shut. He had not paid any attention to Charlie's glasses. Fitzhugh took out his cell phone and started to dial a number. "Just punch it in," directed Charlie. "Let me do the talking." He did so and handed the phone to Charlie who checked and memorized the number on the screen as he drew it to his ear, holding it far enough way so that his glasses could pick up the sound. On the second ring a female voice answered.

"Vanderpool Enterprises."

"Mr. Vanderpool, please."

"I'm sorry. Mr. Vanderpool is unavailable."

"I'm Charlie Jenkins. I'm sitting here with a man who says he's Lester Fitzhugh. I need to speak to Mr. Vanderpool."

There was a pause and then, "One moment, please. I will transfer you."

There was a long pause and some switching clicks and then a male voice. "I'm Mr. Vanderpool's private assistant. You say you're Mr. Jenkins and you're with Mr. Fitzhugh?"

"That's correct."

"Let me speak with Mr. Fitzhugh."

Charlie handed the phone across the table. "He wants to talk to you." Charlie could only hear one end of the conversation.

"Yeah, it's me. . . . I know the boss doesn't like to do this . . . . I can't help it. He insists . . . . We won't get anything done if he doesn't . . . . Yeah, he's clean. I checked him . . . . " There was a long pause. "Yeah, I'll put him on." He handed the phone back to Charlie. Another male voice came on the line.

"You're Mr. Jenkins?"

"That's right. And who are you?" Charlie had determined to rankle Vanderpool a little

"You know damned good and well I'm J. Pat Vanderpool." There was anger in his voice.

"Then you're the father of that little pervert who tried to molest my granddaughter." Charlie could hear a breath being sucked in and Vanderpool trying to control his voice.

"Jason is my son, yes."

"What do we need to talk about?"

"Mr. Jenkins, let me say that Mr. Fitzhugh handles all my negotiations."

"Are you telling me that he will be speaking for you in any terms he might propose?"

"That is correct."

"And you will honor any terms he makes?"

"That is also correct."

"Thank you for your time, Mr. Vanderpool. It's been nice talking to you." Charlie shut the phone and handed it back. "Your move," he said to Fitzhugh.

"Let's eat as we talk," said Fitzhugh, as he picked up his sandwich. "We've investigated you quite thoroughly. Both you and your wife are retired. Your home is paid for as are your two cars. Your income is adequate but not excessive. Your daughter's marriage has failed and she's back with you until she can get back on her feet. This could be a golden opportunity for you to ensure her and your granddaughter's financial future, college, professional school, and so on."

Campbell had cautioned Charlie about getting close to agreeing to any pay-off until they got Jason arraigned. "You mean you wanna pay me off to let that little pervert walk free so he can molest some more little girls?"

"Please, Mr. Jenkins, we would prefer to say that you're just procuring a little insurance for your family's future."

"How big of a policy are we talking about?"

"Let's say well into six figures."

"How well into?'

"Possibly 500,000. That's the limit."

"Two things, Mr. Fitzhugh. First of all, I think that little bastard is a menace to society and I'm not inclined to let him off the hook. Secondly, if and I say IF, I were inclined to cash your insurance policy, 500 is not an adequate return."

Fitzhugh finished the last bite of his sandwich before speaking. "Then this meeting is terminated. We'll be back in touch." He put enough cash on the table to cover the tab, dumped Charlie's valuables out of the sack onto the table, and took his leave.

Charlie got his stuff back into his pockets, adjusted his glasses, and left. A nondescript man a few tables over who had been eating and reading the Wall Street Journal followed him out to the parking lot and stood watching as he drove away.

When Charlie got home, he called Detective Campbell who was ecstatic about the meeting. He said that Vanderpool had come in loud and clear and that with all the recordings of his voice at council meetings, they would not have any problem making a comparative voice print to prove it was him on the phone. "We never thought you'd get him to talk to you right off the bat, but you did. However, you did push him a little hard. We don't want to piss him off too much."

"Okay. I'll back off a little," said Charlie.

Campbell went on, "Now, let's have a little strategy session for your next meeting. It'll be soon. Jason will be well enough for the preliminary hearing in a week or so. We're sure Vanderpool wants you out of the picture before then so we'll have to drop the case. We cannot give him any glimmer that that's gonna happen." The two talked on for several minutes. Charlie felt a sense of pride. He might be old but he'd just turned in a good day's work.

Campbell was right. Fitzhugh called three days later and set the meeting for lunch at The Saddle Horn Steak House. "You still buying?" Charlie asked. Fitzhugh responded by hanging up on him. "These people have no sense of humor," he told Suzy as he called Campbell.

The meeting started with a trip to the bathroom, a full body search, and pocket contents into the bag. "Why don't I just certify I'm clean and we could avoid all this?" A grunt was Fitzhugh's only comment.

After they ordered Fitzhugh got right down to business. "Mr. Jenkins, we hope you realize that you have a very weak case."

"The DA doesn't think so."

"Well, our attorneys do. You see, your only witnesses are an elderly man and a little girl. Our attorneys will tear you two apart. There's no surveillance tape. The judge might not even bind Jason over. If he doesn't, everything goes up in smoke. My employer doesn't want either side to have to go through a lot of messy public legal stuff. That's why he's willing to forego bringing assault charges against you and is making you a generous insurance policy offer."

Charlie was seething inside but he tried not to show it. His voice was steady. "What's the 'policy' worth today?"

"He thinks 750 is a very generous number."

"I don't give a rat's ass what he thinks. It's what I think that counts and I think he'd not in the ballpark yet."

Fitzhugh sat back and looked at Charlie for a long moment before speaking. "Mr. Jenkins, I think you're gambling. You're gambling that the judge will bind the boy over and that your departure price will escalate afterwards. Do not gamble with us. You are way out of your league."

"I really hadn't thought of that angle," replied Charlie, "but it is something to consider."

"And let me point out something else," Fitzhugh went on, "you're an old man. These legal matters can drag on for quite some time. You might not live to see them resolved."

"Oh, I'm in pretty good health except for that Chinese metal in my back."

"But, you know, a man your age could die most anytime."

"That sounds a little like a threat, Mr. Fitzhugh."

"Oh, no. I just feel that it's my duty to point out all facets of the issue. The 750 is still on the table."

"It'll just have to stay there. I'm not gonna pick it up."

Their food came. "It will stay there until I leave. It will go with me. Beyond that there's nothing else to discuss." The men ate is silence.

Charlie called Campbell when he got home. The detective was pleased with the meeting. "What do you think about that threat?' asked Charlie.

"Well, he's never hurt or killed anyone in the past but we haven't had him by the balls like this before."

"I've got a carry permit. You think I ought to start packing?"

"That's up to you. Just don't do anything stupid."

That afternoon Charlie was at the kitchen table cleaning his pistol when Suzy walked by,

"What's this?" she asked.

"Just a little insurance, my dear," he replied, "just a little insurance."

* * *

There was a crowd at the preliminary hearing. Jason Vanderpool was pushed in in a wheel chair, looking like death warmed over. "He's wearing makeup," whispered Suzy to Charlie.

"Are you sure?"

"Of course, I'm sure. I know makeup when I see it. They're gonna play this victim thing to the hilt."

The case was called. "What's the plea?" asked the judge.

Jason had three lawyers. Fitzhugh was not in sight. One rose and responded, "Your Honor, as you can see, my client has been an innocent victim of a brutal attack. And furthermore...."

The judge cut him off. "Save it for the trial, counselor. Let's have a plea."

"Not guilty, Your Honor."

The judge turned to the DA. "Recommendations for bail."

"The State recommends that the defendant be remanded. He possess adequate resources to flee the Country."

"Your Honor," Jason's attorney broke in, "My client has a clean record, no convictions."

"If you call multiple arrests for similar crimes plus a lengthy juvenile record 'clean,' what would you call 'dirty'?" The DA shot back.

"This on-going harassment of my client has not even produced a trial," the defense attorney countered.

"That's enough, you two." The judge cut them off. "Bail is set at one million dollars. The defendant will surrender his passport." The gavel came down hard. "Next case."

For the first time, Charlie looked at J. Patton Vanderpool who was seated in the first row behind the defense table. They made eye contact. There was pure hate in his eyes. Charlie got an uneasy feeling in the pit of his stomach. "Expect some more pressure," warned Detective Campbell as they left the courtroom.

Three days later, 10:00 AM, a call came from Fitzhugh. "It's time to talk again" he said. "Use your wife's car today. Give me your cell number. Drive west on Colmore. I'll call and direct you as you go."

Charlie immediately called Campbell. "They're guarding against a tracking device on your car but we've got that covered. We'll be close. Just be careful."

As Charlie drove along Colmore, his cell rang. "Where are

you?" asked Fitzhugh. Charlie told him. "Good. Turn left on Prospect." He did so and soon another call came. "Take a right on Hubbard." Charlie began to feel uneasy. He placed his pistol in the passenger seat with a newspaper over it. He was getting into an industrial district. Another call. "Take a left on Bates." Charlie knew that Bates would take him down close to the river in a seedy warehouse district. He pulled the car over. "Just where are you taking me?" he asked. "There're no restaurants in this area."

"Oh, we are not doing a restaurant today. I thought a more private location would be more conducive to our negotiations."

"Well, it's gonna be real private because you're gonna be by yourself. I will never meet with you in a 'private' place, only in broad daylight in a public place." Charlie snapped his phone shut, made a U-turn and headed for home. He called Campbell on the way and filled him in.

"We were wondering where you were headed. You made a smart move. Vanderpool probably had some of his goons set to rough you up some. Just be real careful. You'll hear from them again."

* * *

A week went by. No calls from Fitzhugh. It was mid-afternoon when the doorbell rang. Suzy went to a window where she could see the front and peeked through the blinds. "It's two men I've never seen before," she reported.

Charlie put on his jacket and went to the door. A look through the peep hole confirmed Suzy's observation. The doorbell rang again. The man on Charlie's right stood a little behind the other with his right arm hidden from view. "What do you want?" he asked through the door.

"Detective Campbell sent us. There're something we need to go over with you" replied the one on the left.

"Do you have badges?" asked Charlie.

Both held up badges in their left hands. They looked just like badges that Campbell and the other detectives wore. Charlie knew the glass storm door was locked so he opened the main door and stood with his right hand in his jacket pocket. There was only a slight movement of the man's hidden arm and the silencer-tipped pistol began its journey to the horizontal. Charlie reacted quickly. The front of his jacket exploded twice shattering the storm door and making two holes in the man's chest. He was dead before he hit the floor. The other gunman was pulling his weapon from his shoulder holster when Charlie's third shot shattered his wrist and continued into his torso. As he went down, blood began to come from his mouth. Charlie could tell he wasn't dead but resisted the temptation to shoot him again. He could hear Suzy screaming and running toward him. She threw her arms around him screaming, "Are you alright! Are you alright!" and then looking in horror at the two crumpled figures on her front stoop.

"Better call 911, dear," said Charlie. "We've got another mess on our hands."

Soon their world turned into another zoo. Police cars with lights flashing, ambulances with their red lights and sirens, policemen all over the place, crime scene tape backup, two TV crews, a whole crowd of gawking onlookers. Fortunately, Connie had taken Sam for a play date that afternoon. Charlie and Suzy sat together in the family room as the chaos swirled around them. Detective Hernandez came and took their statements. After a while things got calmer and Detective Campbell came in.

"First of all, I want to apologize for almost getting you killed. We've had a surveillance team on you all at night but we just never figured they'd try something in broad daylight."

"I'm not blaming you," Charlie replied.

"I know you're not but I still feel bad about it. From now on we'll have some one on you around the clock. Looking back, I'd say they intended to kill you a week ago down by the river."

"What about these two? Their badges looked real."

"They were. They belong to two of our offices who 'loaned' them out. That's totally against regulations. They'll probably be dismissed. Oh, by the way, I'll need your gun and jacket for evidence. I kinda hate to take your pistol."

"That's okay. I've got another one. What about the two I shot?"

"One was dead at the scene. The bullet that hit the other one got slowed down going through his wrist bones so it didn't kill him. He's in critical condition. There's a pretty good chance he'll live."

"Are they some of Vanderpool's strong arm boys?"

"No. They're not. I'll tell you what we've been able to piece together so far. They're from Chicago and the Chicago Police Department sends their thanks to you for removing two of their problems. The car was a rental. In it we found round trip plane tickets and a manila envelope containing your picture and directions to your house. The badges probably were in the envelope as well.

"What are the chances you'll get the live one to talk?" asked Charlie.

"Probably slim and none. And even if we do, he may not even know who hired him and didn't want to know. These hired guns usually get so much down and the rest after the job is done. The money will be hard to track. We're trying to find out who rented the car."

"What's next?" Charlie asked.

"That's what we need to talk about. You are obviously in danger. We've got some charges on Vanderpool we think will stick but we'd like to have more. If you want to quit this cloak and dagger stuff, we'll understand and go with what we've got."

"Even if I quit doing the tapes, I'm still gonna be in as much danger, am I not?"

"Well, yes, I'd say so."

"Then let's go on. I'd like to hang ole J. Pat up by his balls just as much as you would." The two men went to a back bedroom and talked for a while.

Fitzhugh called the next day on Charlie's cell phone. Charlie turned on his glasses. "My employer sends his sincere apology," he began. Charlie could hardly believe his ears. "One of his ambitious employees overstepped his bounds and ordered something which he would never condone."

"If you think I believe that, you're full of shit."

"He understands how you must feel but hopes that this has not cut off your willingness to negotiate."

Charlie paused a moment before replying. "It has not. But the rules have changed. From here on in, I'm calling the shots. I will tell you where and when we will meet. If you cannot accept that, you and your employer can go to hell."

"We should be able to handle that."

"Then our next meeting is at Stoney River Steak House at one thirty this coming Tuesday."

"I have it on my calendar," Fitzhugh replied. Charlie shut his phone.

Campbell called a few days later. "Bad news," he said. "We've lost Jason."

"What do you mean 'lost'?" Charlie asked.

"I mean he's flown the coop, jumped bail."

"How in the world did that happen?"

"It happened because we didn't have him in jail and could only watch him to a certain degree. It happened because J. Pat has a lot of connections and resources."

"Do you have any idea where he is?"

"We suspect he left the country by private jet and is in some Caribbean country which has no extradition treaty with us."

"How's this gonna effect my meeting with Fitzhugh?"

"That's hard to say. If he doesn't contact you, keep the appointment and see what happens."

* * *

Fitzhugh was waiting for him. They went through the obligatory "wire check, put things in the bag" exercise. Fitzhugh was surprised when Charlie put a pistol in the bag. "They do come in handy sometime," he said. Fitzhugh just shrugged.

After they ordered Fitzhugh opened the conversation. "I assume you are aware that Mr. Vanderpool, Jr. decided to change his place of residence while awaiting the solution to his problems.

"I am aware that he jumped bail. How is this going to affect your employer's willingness to resolve the issue?"

"No change there. He would like to make sure that the boy can come back with no cloud hanging over him."

"Good. There're some things you and Vanderpool need to understand. First of all, you are two very lucky people. You didn't discover that I was trained as a crack sniper. With a rifle and a good scope I can decide which of your eyes to shoot out at 500 yards. There're several in my old outfit still around who have maintained their skills through the years. I've called them to help me in this and they jumped at the chance. They have had you two marked for a good while now. If those goons from Chicago had killed me the other day, neither you nor your boss would have lived to see the sun go down. That's what I mean when I say you are two very lucky people. And furthermore, if anything happens to any of my family, especially Sam, you two won't live 24 hours." Fitzhugh had begun to look around apprehensively. "And don't worry. It'll be quick. You'll never know what hit you. Of course, if anybody's close to you, they'll have to clean your brains off their clothes."

Fitzhugh's voice was a little shaky as he spoke. "I don't think you're kidding."

"I'm not. Vanderpool thinks I'm just some little nobody he can push around. I may be a nobody but I don't push very easily. You see, I fought for this country and survived the Korean War and if you think I'm going to roll over and play dead for some sorry bastard like J. Patton Vanderpool, you'd better think again. Do we understand each other on that?"

"Yes, I think we do."

"Okay. Now this whole thing has gotten totally out of hand. Personally, I'd like to see both Vanderpool and his son rot in jail. But there's another aspect. I don't care about myself but I would like to ensure the futures of my daughter and granddaughter. So I'm gonna do that. The price is two million - one million now and one when everything is settled. And if the second million doesn't come I can always go the other way."

"That's quite a sum of money," observed Fitzhugh.

"It is but Vanderpool's not going to go hungry from it. He can just count it as his contribution to the betterment of society."

"I'll see what I can do . . .uh, see what my employer says about it."

"No. You won't just 'see', you will 'do'. None of this is subject to negotiations, and furthermore, I want Vanderpool to bring the money. I want to look him in the eye on this."

"Oh, he would never agree to that."

"If he wants his son back, he will agree."

"He can't afford to be recognized."

"Then he needs to come in disguise. He's completely bald. Get a wig. Wear dark glasses. Put on a fake beard. Surely he's got some people who can fix him up."

"I will discuss the matter with him."

Their sandwiches came. Charlie took a bite of his. "That's good. He has eight days. I'll meet him at Barron's Bistro on the 22nd at 11:30. You come, too."

Fitzhugh put some money on the table to cover the check. "I've lost my appetite," he said as he put the bag with Charlie's stuff on the table.

"It's lonely eating alone," said Charlie.

"I'm sure you'll manage," Fitzhugh said as he got to his feet.

Charlie reached into the bag and drew out his cell. "You need to remember one thing. If I dial a number on this, you won't get home tonight."

Fitzhugh left without responding. He turned at the door and looked back. Charlie waved the cell phone at him. He darted out the door glancing in all directions.

After finishing his sandwich, Charlie called Campbell. "Did you get everything?"

"Loud and clear. But listen, you should have told me about those snipers you've got stalking these folks. We can't have that."

"Don't worry," laughed Charlie, "there are no snipers. I just made that up. I wanted to throw a little scare into ole J. Pat."

"Good Lord. And I was worried you couldn't act. We'll talk before the 22nd."

"Sure thing," said Charlie as he closed the phone.

* * *

Charlie got to Barron's early. He had called ahead and reserved a table in one of the little alcoves. He took the gunfighter's seat and waited. They were right on time. Fitzhugh was carrying an attaché case. Vanderpool did indeed have on a wig, mustache and dark glasses. Both were grim-faced. Fitzhugh handed the case to Charlie who put it in the chair beside him. They sat down across the table. "You gentlemen don't look happy today," Charlie said.

"We're not here to make small talk," Vanderpool growled. "Just verify the merchandise."

Charlie popped the two catches and opened the top a few inches. He'd never seen so much cash stacked so neatly all in one place. "Should I count it" he asked.

"It's all there," Vanderpool said. "You have my word on that."

"I'm sure your word is something I can really count on," replied Charlie, his voice dripping with sarcasm.

"Don't try to get all moralistic on me," snarled Vanderpool. "You're no better than I am."

Charlie sat looking at Vanderpool for several seconds before replying. "I suppose you could be right," he said as he removed his glasses and laid them on the table.

At this signal a man and woman who had been dining across the room got up and came to stand behind the two men. Their eyes widened in disbelief when one of the detectives said, "You are both under arrest. Put your hands behind your backs. You have the right to remain silent...."

* * *

Charlie and Suzy went to Vanderpool's preliminary hearing. He had the same three attorneys who had represented his son. They were before the same judge. When the case was called, the DA stood and read a whole litany of charges - one of which was attempted murder. Campbell had managed to tie the car rental to him. "How do you plead?" the judge asked.

One of his lawyers spoke. "Your honor, my client is one of the pillars of this community...."

The judge cut him off. "I didn't ask for his resume, just his plea. What is it?"

"Not guilty, your Honor."

"Thank you. Recommendations for bail."

The DA said, "Your Honor, we ask that he be remanded. Mr. Vanderpool has vast resources and could easily flee the country.

The defense attorney broke in. "Your Honor, my client has no record other than a couple of parking tickets. He is a long-time member of the City Council. He is ...."

The judge cut him off. "Counselor, I seem to remember that you recently had a client with this same name. I set a high bail but he is now nowhere to be found. I'm not going to get bitten in the butt twice by the same family. The prisoner is remanded."

"But, your Honor." The lawyer was almost shouting.

"Counselor, I said 'remanded.' Surely I don't have to spell and define it for you." The gavel came down. "Next case."

Charlie and Suzy looked at each other. Maybe there was a little justice after all.

* * *

About two weeks after Vanderpool's arraignment, Charlie opened the morning paper to have a blaring headline jump out at him: "Local Fugitive Hacked To Death in the Caribbean." The article related how a local sugar cane farmer had caught Jason in the act of molesting his ten-year-old daughter, had grabbed up his cane-cutting machete, and had hacked the boy to death. The account went on to say that the famer did such a thorough job that the authorities were not sure they had found all the parts he chopped off. The farmer was being hailed a local hero. It was unclear whether the body would be sent back to the U. S.

He showed the article to Suzy. "Well, he won't bother any more little girls," was her observation.

"You're right about that," replied Charlie. "Ole J. Pat's problems just seem to be mounting up. I'd hate to be in his shoes."

* * *

Three days later they had just finished dinner. Charlie was helping Suzy load the dishwasher. Connie was getting Sam a bath and ready for bed. The phone rang. It was Detective Campbell. The conversation did not last long. When Charlie hung up the phone, Suzy knew something was wrong. "What now?" she asked. There was apprehension in her voice.

"They just found Vanderpool dead in his cell," Charlie answered. "He hanged himself with a bed sheet." Charlie turned and went out the back door. The whole scene didn't seem real to

Suzy. The sound of Sam playing in the tub came from down the hall. She realized she was holding a dirty plate and made herself finish her table-clearing task before going out to see about her husband. She found him sitting on the patio, staring off into space. "What's wrong, dear?" she asked.

After a while he spoke. "You know, Honey, all this has been a hell of a mess. Sam got traumatized, several members of the Police Department have lost their careers and may go to jail, I killed one man and almost killed another, Jason got hacked to death, Vanderpool took his own life. It sort of makes you wonder."

"About what, dear?"

"Wonder what would have happened if we'd just taken the money?"

Suzy sat down on the arm of Charlie's chair and put an arm across his shoulders. "That's not the man I've been married to for 45 years talking now. You know we did the right thing."

"Yes. But unfortunately the 'right thing' doesn't pay very well," responded Charlie. "I'd just like to be able to give Connie and Sam a secure future.

"You've given them a lot more than you think. And you know if you'd taken that bribe, you'd never be able to live with yourself and I wouldn't want to live with you. Connie and Sam are going to be fine. Connie's tough. She's got a good job. She's a good mother. We'll help in other ways. I don't want to hear any more talk like that from you. Promise me that." She leaned down and kissed him on the cheek.

"Okay, it's a promise," he said. Suzy slid down into the chair beside him and they sat together in silence, enjoying the comfortable feeling that 45 years brings.

They were interrupted by the phone's ringing. News had gotten out about J. Pat and a reporter wanted an interview. Charlie turned him down. Then, the phone began to ring almost constantly with interview requests. All were turned down. A TV reporter with camera came to the door. Charlie sent him away. The phone continued to ring. Finally, Charlie exploded, "I'm so tired of all this crap I could puke," he shouted as he turned off the phone and disconnected the doorbell. Neither slept well.

The next morning and after Connie left to take Sam to school, Charlie turned the phone back on. Calls for interviews were all rebuffed. Suzy busied herself with household chores and let Charlie handle the callers. Most only lasted a few seconds because Charlie wasn't about to give any interviews. But then, on one call Charlie talked for several minutes. After he hung up, he came into where Suzy was making their bed. He had an odd look on his face.

"Is something wrong, dear?" she asked.

"You'll never guess who just called," he said. "That was a fellow from Doubleday publishing house. He's talking six figures - well up in six figures - with the possibility of movie rights after that."

Suzy was so stunned she couldn't speak. She just stood holding a pillow like she didn't know where to put it.

"And you know what the best part is?" Charlie asked.

"What?"

Charlie smiled for the first time. "It's honest money."

The Great Catapult Caper

Lee went to high school at a college prep school for boys in Tennessee. This fiasco began in 1971 during his freshman year in Mr. Kent's advanced Latin class. Mr. Kent was a scholar who spoke fluent Latin and was somewhat odd in other ways as well. One day in the fall of the year he began class with a question: "Boys, how would you all like to build a Roman catapult?" The answer was a resounding "yes." It was to be a class project in which all would participate and all would receive a grade. And so the wheels were set in motion.

Research was done on various types of these machines and the principles involved. There was no budget so all materials would have to be begged or scrounged. One student knew someone who had access to used railroad crossties. These would be the frame work, making it a very heavy device. Another student "procured" a 30-foot telephone pole for the throwing arm. Someone at the School had connections with a bridge company in Nashville which donated some materials as well as fabricated the counter-weights. These were large circular concrete pieces with round holes in the center which could be slipped over the base of the throwing arm. More weight on the base increased the force of the throw. Only hand tools were to be used, making the construction a long, slow process. In fact the construction took the rest of the school year. But by spring it was completed and test fired. To everyone's amazement, it worked. As far as the boys were concerned, the project had been completed. However, they did not realize the saga of the catapult was just beginning.

When the 1972 school year opened, most of the same boys were in the next level of advanced Latin. Mr. Kent came with a new announcement: "Boys, the School has given us permission to attend the National High School Catapult Competition in Indianapolis, Indiana, in the spring." They'd never heard of such but they were eager to go. This would mean a whole new set of problems to solve.

Since the School would provide no budget, how would they get there and where would they stay? After much negotiation the Headmaster agreed to assign one of the School's buses to transport the 18 students and their teacher. And they would camp on the competition grounds. So the boys rounded up tents and camping supplies.

Too large and heavy to be moved in one piece, the catapult would have to be taken apart and reassembled. But how would they haul all the heavy pieces? Some parent had a connection somewhere and from a local National Guard or Reserve Unit, there materialized a low-boy truck with driver. The juxtaposition of this ancient siege weapon and U. S. 20th century military was hardly lost on Mr. Kent.

And Mr. Kent insisted that each participant be in authentic dress with spear and/or sword. Each boy fashioned his own weapons and their mothers made the costumes. Lee's mother made him one of those knee-length Roman skirts with vertical leather strips.

By April everything was in place. The mammoth machine had been christened OTUS and EPHIALTUS and this cohort of Tennessee Romans headed north.

The competition area was a 10-acre field. There were 22 teams, mostly from New England and the mid-west. Theirs' was the only Southern team so the boys hung Rebel flags from their tents. (Remember this was almost 50 years ago.) An incident in setting up camp was a portent of the next few days. One of the boys was chopping firewood when he embedded the axe in the top of his foot. He took off his boot and poured blood out on the ground, saying, "Mr. Kent, I think I need to go the hospital." His teacher spread the cut sock, surveyed the wound, and poured about half a bottle of alcohol over his foot. He almost passed out from the pain. Mr. Kent wrapped the foot up in the bloody sock, saying, "You'll be okay."

In his book on the history of this competition, Dr. B. F. Barcio likens it to an ancient field of combat and says of this incident: "...cries pierced the night as a zealous wood chopper drove an ax into his own foot and christened the field with blood."

The next faux pas came with the reassembly. The long, heavy throwing arm (telephone pole) had to be walked up into place by several boys. Somehow it got out of balance and came crashing down. The boys scattered. Lee was running backward and fell over a crosstie. The pole struck him on one side of his face. Fortunately, no bones were broken but his teeth shredded his cheek on the inside and made one small hole to the exterior. The cheek felt like limber stalactites to his tongue. He said, "Mr. Kent, I think I need to go to the hospital." After surveying the injury Mr. Kent replied, "You've just got one small hole. Use some mouth wash. You'll be okay." Lee was beginning to see a pattern to his teacher's diagnoses.

The pole had also fallen on another boy's knee. He said, "I think I need to go to the hospital." After the injury was checked, everyone was surprised when Mr. Kent said, "You know, I think you're right," and sent him for medical attention.

As they observed the other teams adjusting their machines and doing practice throws, their team soon figured they were out-classed. Some of these sleek, professional looking catapults were throwing rocks almost out of sight. But Mr. Kent came up with a winning strategy. "Boys," he directed, "go find a very big rock." "How big?" someone asked. "So big that you almost cannot move it," he answered. "Our only hope to compete is to throw something really big in the heavyweight division." No one remembers where they got the big rock but it weighed in at 335 pounds.

The spring nights were cold - so cold that the boys used kerosene heaters in their tents. Whether it was the cold or the mouth wash (maybe both), Lee's jaw began to feel better even though that side of his face was about twice the size of the other.

On the night before the competition, there came an eerie, mournful sound in the camp. Mr. Kent had consumed a little too much alcohol, exited his tent, and was howling at the moon. From all that had happened so far, Lee was not sure that this was an auspicious sign.

The next day was a flurry of activity. There was throwing, measuring, and cheering from all quarters. This was covered by several national news organizations. Their team passed on all the early throws, pinning their hope on "the big rock." Finally they were on stage.

All the other teams had thrown. No other team was attempting such a weight so all eyes were on them. They loaded on all the counter weights, cranked the arm down, and loaded the boulder into the projectile cradle. The two-inch diameter hawser rope was stretched tight. Lee was the trigger man. He took his machete and slashed at the rope. It just bounced off. All the weight had stretched the rope, making it as hard a steel. It was Mr. Kent who saw a solution. He stood, pointed to the tents, and shouted in his best Shakespearean Roman oratorical voice, "Fetch the kerosene. We'll burn it." The burning rope did not give way immediately. There were small pops as fibers burned and snapped. Suddenly critical mass was reached, the rope parted, and the rock was flung into space. The distance was a winning 43 feet.

But their victory celebration was short-lived. The kerosene and the fire had spread to the flammable, creosoted crossties. With no means to put it out, they stood by and watched OTUS and EPHIALTUS burn to the ground. However, one positive aspect was that they did not have to take it apart and haul it home.

A trophy was presented signifying that their School was the 1973 National High School Catapult Champion - Heavyweight Division, making it the only national team championship the School has ever won in its 130-year history. Unfortunately, over time the trophy has been lost and the memory of this achievement has faded away. Perhaps the School will take steps to rectify this and give this team its well-deserved recognition.

The trip home was uneventful. Since Lee's face seemed to be healing, his mother did not send him to a doctor. The wood chopper's foot healed also as did the boy's knee. However, when the new school year opened in the fall, Mr. Kent was not on the faculty. His contract had not been renewed. Nobody knew whether or not the catapult or his howling at the moon or his medical diagnoses had anything to do with his departure.

In reflecting on this episode, one can note that even the selection of OTUS and EPHIALTUS as names for the catapult was significant and prophetic.   In mythology these two were enormous twin sons of Poseidon. They spent their time creating mischief for the other gods.   Could any other names be so apropos?

"The Great Catapult Caper

One student places his life in the hands of his teammates as he adjusts the throwing arm's projectile cradle.

The Loser

He was not a bad kid. He was tall, slender, and good looking with a pleasing personality—sort of the all-American boy. One had to wonder how this tenth grader had gotten himself so far off track to be expelled from boarding school. But he had. And now here he was—exiled to his dorm room allowed to leave only for the bathroom and meals—waiting for his father to come for him the next day; waiting, with his clothes packed; waiting, forbidden to talk to anyone; waiting, and reflecting; waiting, and lonely. Just waiting.

It all started a couple of months earlier. He had been caught smoking pot and given a second chance because he'd not brought any on campus nor had he enticed or supplied it to anyone else. He'd promised to quit and he really wanted to. Perhaps he could have done so with a good treatment and counseling program. But at that time there were none available, so he was relegated to doing it on his own—something he could not do. Expulsion was to be the penalty for another offense. The outcome was predictable.

I sat in my office waiting for his father, reflecting on the situation. His parents were divorced. His father who had custody had remarried and sent him off to boarding school. He was a follower who desperately wanted to be accepted. Unfortunately, he had followed the wrong people and picked the wrong route to acceptance. His mother was out of the picture.

This boy had spent a goodly portion of his life dealing with rejection. And now his school was rejecting him. I wished we could have done something else but we had no other options. The phone call to his father had been a hard one. I dreaded the face-to-face meeting which was imminent.

My phone buzzed. I heard the dreaded words from my secretary, "Mr. Perry is here."

"Send him in and send someone to the dorm to get Bill."

I rose as he entered. We shook hands. It was obvious he was not in a good mood. "I'm sorry," I began.

He cut me off. "Don't be sorry. It's not your fault. I don't know what I'm going to do with that kid. I send him off to a good school and this is the thanks I get. He'll probably wind up a pot-head living under a bridge someplace."

I offered him a chair but he indicated he'd rather stand. He continued to pace about my office as he talked about the situation.

"He's really cost me some money this time and I don't mean the lost tuition. I was in the middle of a big business deal and he picks this time to screw up. I like to have never gotten all those people together and I had to walk out in the middle of everything. I'm sure the deal's kaput now."

It was an awkward situation. I thought I knew what Bill needed but it was obvious his father didn't want to hear from me—or anyone else, for that matter. It seemed to me that he was the type person who had all the answers—or thought he did.

Bill walked—or rather slunk—in. He was all slumped over and looked like a whipped puppy. He stood by the doorway waiting for his father to notice him. His eyes were red from crying. He needed someone to put his arms around him but I had the feeling this need wouldn't be met.

His father noticed him and halted in mid stride. His voice

dripped with sarcasm when he spoke. "Well, here you are. You know something? You're nothing but a loser. Yep, nothing but a loser." Bill flinched like he'd been shot.

Mr. Perry stood looking at his son. Although only about eight feet of space separated them, they were miles apart. Bill could not meet his father's gaze. He began to cry.

Mr. Perry moved toward the door. "Quit your sniveling and let's go load up. I've got work to get back to." By this time he was out the door. He had not touched his son.

Bill turned to follow his father. I couldn't let him leave like that. I grabbed his arm, turned him around, and looked him in the eye. "Son, I'm going to tell you something and I don't want you ever to forget it. Nobody can make you a loser unless you let 'em. Will you remember that?"

"Yes sir, I'll remember." I released my grip and he left.

It's been over twenty-five years now. I have not seem nor heard from the Perrys since that day. I still think about Bill every once in a while—and wonder if he ever became a winner.

A Quid Pro Quo?

> "It is the eternal struggle between these two principles
> - right and wrong
> - throughout the world."
> --Abraham Lincoln

January 1948 at The Winslow School

It was the first class day of the second semester and the teachers had gone over the exams from the first term and given out the grades. Lance was pleased with his As in Biology and Geometry and Bs in Latin and English. But he was concerned about Shark who was repeating the whole Freshman year.

After supper he went down to Shark's room to see how he'd done. The door was closed. He knocked and Shark yelled for him to come in. He was at his desk working on his algebra. Shark was one of the few boys who started studying before the study hour bell.

"Well, how'd you do?" asked Lance.

Shark seemed to swell with pride as he answered, "Passed 'em all."

"That's great!" exclaimed Lance slapping Shark on the back so hard that he almost knocked the breath out of him. "That's just a little better than last year. What are your grades?"

"All Cs and proud to have 'em," responded Shark, "considering I never had one passing grade last year on anything. You know my daddy said I'd be here until I graduated if it took twenty years. I'm trying to cut that down some," Shark joked.

"I'm sure your folks will be proud of you," said Lance.

"Yep, I'm sure they will. They may even think they've got a future scholar on their hands." Shark paused for a few seconds looking closely at Lance. "I don't guess you've heard about Train," Shark said hesitantly.

"Oh, good Lord," responded Lance the disgust showing in his voice. "Don't tell me he flunked Biology."

"That's what I hear."

Lance sat down on Shark's bed and began pummeling the pillow with his fist. "Damn, damn, damn. There goes our baseball season. And with everybody trying to help that guy. Are you sure?"

"Well, he didn't tell me but I got it pretty straight."

"I'm gonna find out for myself," said Lance as he jumped up and headed for Train's room in Madison Hall.

Train's door was open and he was stretched out on his bed listening to the radio. Lance barged in without knocking. "Is it true?" he asked.

"Is what true?" responded Train. He seemed unconcerned.

"That you flunked Biology."

"Yep. It's true. Sure did," replied Train as adjusted the radio dial.

"I guess you just don't give a shit," responded Lance obviously agitated. "Mr. Sherman offered to let you do some make-up work over Christmas and you wouldn't even take your book home. I offered to tutor you and you said you didn't need it. And you just sat around on your ass and flunked. Without you to pitch, our baseball season is in the toilet."

"Aw, don't get your bowels in such an uproar," Train admonished as he continued to fiddle with the radio. "All is under control. I'll be on the mound come opening game."

"How in hell you think you're gonna pull that off? You've flunked a course! You know you've got to pass all your courses to be eligible."

"Well, you know, Lance, there's just something you country boys don't understand." Train's voice had a condescending tone. "Grades can be changed. I talked to my old man on the phone this afternoon. He'll be here at the end of the week to take care of things."

"You've lost your cotton-picking mind!" said Lance his voice rising in volume. "If I thought it'd do any good, I'd take your ass to the woods and stomp it in the ground!" Lance turned on his heel and stalked out of the room. Train was still adjusting the radio.

* * *

The next day Coach Buck sent a note to Train asking him to come by his office during his open period. Train sauntered through the open door without knocking and flopped down in a chair in front of Coach Buck's desk. "You wanted to see me, Coach?" Train asked.

Coach Buck sat studying the boy for a long moment before speaking. "That's right, son. I saw the grades yesterday." His words were measured; his tone sharp. "I couldn't help but notice that you failed Biology which makes you ineligible for baseball this spring. Could you explain to me how you managed to pull that off with everyone bending over backward to help you? You've let everybody down including yourself."

Train had begun to squirm a little under the force of Coach Buck's words. "Don't worry, sir. I've got it covered." There was the hint of a swagger in Train's voice.

Coach Buck's eyes narrowed as he leaned forward. "What do you mean 'you've got it covered?' You couldn't cover your butt with a fifty-foot tarp." His words dripped with sarcasm.

"My father will be here at the end of the week. He's gonna take care of it," answered Train.

"Maybe you could let me in on just how he's gonna accomplish this. Is he gonna wave a magic wand over your head and all of a sudden you're gonna know all the bones of the human body or what osmosis is, none of which you were willing to learn for Mr. Sherman? Or maybe he's gonna pass some other type of miracle. How about you let me in on the secret."

"Well, sir, my father made a lot of money during the war. From just looking around, I'd say Winslow could use some of it. I'm sure he and Mr. Breckenridge will be able to come to an understanding."

Coach Buck leaned back in his chair and looked at Train in disbelief - and then in anger. "Son, you are an idiot if you think that's gonna happen. Even IF your daddy managed to pull that off, I'm still the coach and I'm telling you right how you'll never put on a uniform for me this spring."

Train seemed to take that pronouncement by Coach Buck as a challenge as he replied, "Well, sir, you know a coach that wouldn't play an eligible player and especially one whose father gave a lot of money to the school just might not be the coach when baseball season gets here."

Coach Buck couldn't believe his ears. His first reaction was disbelief and then anger - intense anger. He was so angry he could not speak. Both hands on the desk top clenched into hard fists. The muscles in his arms and shoulders expanded and rippled as if they were trying to break out through the shirt's fabric. Train saw the fists, the bulging muscles, and the look on Coach Buck's face. He cut his eyes both ways seeking a route of escape. Coach Buck's first thought was to go over the desk after the boy and slap some sense into him but he controlled that urge. After what seemed like an eternity but which was probably no longer than thirty seconds, Coach Buck was able to open his fists and clasp his hands together. His muscles ceased fighting the shirt's restraint. He leaned forward, fixed Train with a penetrating gaze, and began to speak.

"Son, I want you to listen very carefully to every word I say. I am not going to repeat myself.

First of all, I do not take kindly to being threatened by a two-bit punk who does not know his ass from hole in the ground. Secondly, let's just assume that the Administration takes your daddy's bribe and then fires me for not playing you. Of course, we're just assuming because I don't think that'll happen in a million years but since you brought it up, we'll just assume it happens that way. Now, you'd better pay very close attention to what I'm fixing to say next because I'm gonna tell you what's gonna happen next.

"I would sue your daddy and this school for a very large amount of money. And even though I have vowed never to trade on my uniform or my war record, I'd make an exception here. And when we got to court I'd be on the witness stand in my dress blues with all my medals on the front - not just the ribbons but the medals. I think I'll probably have room for all of them. And right at the top will be that one with the white stars on the blue background. I think you know the one I'm referring to. And who do you think a jury is gonna believe - your side or a war hero with the Congressional Medal of Honor on his chest? And it'll be in all the papers and your daddy will be humiliated and his name won't be worth a plug nickel anywhere in this country. You see, son, I looked death in the face on Guadalcanal and if you think I'm gonna cut and run from the Johnson family, you'd better think again."

Train was getting uneasy. He was beginning to realize that he'd bitten off more than he could chew. He fidgeted in his chair as Coach Buck continued.

"And then, after winning the lawsuit, I'd come find both you and your daddy and kick the living shit outta both of you. In fact, I just might as well get an early jump on that last part and start with you right now." Coach Buck got to his feet as he spoke and started around the desk. Train levitated from the chair, whirled, and bolted out the door. Coach Buck remained standing beside his desk for several seconds with a half-smile on his face.

Coach Buck closed his office door and sat behind his desk for a few minutes, thinking. He then walked over to The Boogers' office and they talked for about thirty minutes. After Coach Buck left, The Booger went across the hall to Headmaster Breckenridge's office. Their session lasted the better part of an hour. Mr. Johnson's pending visit would be a surprise to no one.

* * *

On that Friday The Booger was in his office trying to finish some reports but he found it hard to concentrate on them. He kept looking out his window at the parking lot. Train's father was yet to show up; neither had he called for an appointment. The Booger had really not expected a call. He had Mr. Johnson pegged as a person who would just show up without notice and demand an audience. The Booger was not looking forward to the impending confrontation.

About mid-morning a long, black Cadillac pulled into the parking lot. Its driver was a tall, distinguished looking man wearing a dark, pin-striped suit and a gray Homburg hat. As he headed for the office, The Booger punched the intercom to the Headmaster's office and reported, "Our visitor has arrived."

"I can hardly wait," answered Mr. Breckenridge.

The man strode into the outer office and up to the receptionist's desk. As he handed her his card, he stated forcefully, "I'm the father of one of your students. I need to see the Headmaster. I don't have an appointment but this is important."

The receptionist looked at the card which read, "J. Baresfoot Johnson, Financial Entrepreneur." "Right this way Mr. Johnson," she said as she led him down the hall and into Mr. Breckenridge's office. As she handed Mr. Breckenridge the card she said, "Sir, this is Mr. Johnson, one of our parents," and turning to the visitor, "This is our Headmaster, Mr. Breckenridge." Mr. Breckenridge rose and extended his hand. "Always glad to meet one of our parents," he said. "My pleasure," replied Mr. Johnson. As they shook hands, the receptionist withdrew closing the door. Mr. Breckenridge did not offer his visitor a seat.

"I'll get right to the point," said Mr. Johnson. "I'm here about my son and his baseball eligibility."

"Yes, I believe he mentioned to our Coach that you might be coming. Well, our Assistant Headmaster, Mr. Montague, handles all those issues. You will need to speak with him about this." Mr. Breckenridge's voice was very calm and even.

"I don't deal with people down the line. I always deal with the head man."

"As I said, Mr. Johnson, Mr. Montague handles these matters.

I can assure you that our philosophies are the same. Whatever disposition he makes will be supported by me and will not be changed." Mr. Breckenridge's voice remained the same.

Frustration was beginning to show on Mr. Johnson's face. His voice became louder as he spoke. "I told you I always deal with the top dog and I'm not going to . . ." He stopped as Mr. Breckenridge raised his hand palm out toward him and began to move toward the door.

"Sir, I'm sure your time is valuable as is mine. There's no sense in wasting it with quibbling. If you will just follow me, I will show you to Mr. Montague's office and he will deal with your problem." Mr. Johnson had little choice but to follow. Mr. Breckenridge had never raised his voice or changed his facial expression.

As the two entered The Booger's office, he rose and extended his hand. "Well, Mr. Johnson, it's good to see you again."

"Have we met?" asked Mr. Johnson as they shook hands.

"Yes, last January when you came to enroll Train. I worked out his schedule and gave you all a tour of the campus.

"I'm sorry," replied Mr. Johnson. "I guess I've had my mind on other things."

"That's quite alright. Won't you have a seat?"

Mr. Breckenridge left closing the door. He went to the receptionist's desk and said to her, "Might as well send for the boy."

Before they were settled good in their chairs, Mr. Johnson opened the conversation. "No sense in beating around the bush. I think you know why I'm here.

"Yes, I think I do."

"Well, how about telling me why he's not eligible to play baseball this spring."

"Gladly, sir. Our conference requires that a student pass four classroom courses each semester in order to be eligible the following semester. Train only takes four. He failed one. Therefore, he cannot play this semester."

"Why didn't you see that he passed?" Mr. Johnsons tone was accusatory.

"Because he refused all assistance. He was put on night school and offered tutors and make-up work. He wouldn't do any of it. I've yet to find a way to pour knowledge into a boy's head that refuses to accept it."

"Well, how can the situation be fixed? He's got to play ball this spring."

"It can't be at this point. He's already failed the course."

"Now Mr. Montague, you know that things can always be fixed. Are you aware of Train's lineage? He's Walter Johnson's nephew. He plans on pitching in the majors someday. Scouts are already looking at him They say he's got a lot of potential. Not playing this spring is not an option."

The Booger leaned forward in his chair and looked intently at Mr. Johnson as he spoke. "Not playing is his only option if he remains at Winslow. He is not eligible."

"Who reports these grades?"

"I do."

"To whom do you report?"

"The Conference Commissioner."

"Well, why don't you just fudge a little? Report he passed and let him make it up later. You know your team needs him. He won four games last year as a freshman."

"I'm not about to certify a false report," stated The Booger. "We don't need anybody that badly."

Mr. Johnson sat back in his chair and gazed at The Booger for several seconds. " I was hoping it wouldn't come to this but I guess it has," he said as he reached into an inside coat pocket and drew out a leather-cased checkbook and pen. He flipped it open, signed the top check, tore it out, and placed it on the desk in front of The Booger before speaking. "It's blank. You can fill it

out. There's no limit. I'm sure the School could use a nice 'donation.' My boy needs to be on that team this spring."

The Booger sat looking at the piece of paper for several seconds. Finally, he picked it up and examined it carefully. He even turned it over and surveyed the back. He did not speak. Growing impatient, Mr. Johnson again opened his checkbook. "Maybe you think there won't be anything in there for you. I'll just sign another one and you can fill it out for yourself." He did so and laid the second check on the desk. The Booger picked it up and gave it the same scrutiny as the first as hot anger rose in him. He tried not to show it. He still did not speak.

Mr. Johnson grew nervous in the silence. Finally, he broke it. "Well, what do you say?"

The Booger carefully put both checks together and then calmly tore them in two, put the pieces together and tore them again. He picked up his stapler and stapled all the pieces together twice before handing them back to Mr. Johnson whose mouth had dropped open. "I wouldn't want you to lose any of the pieces," said The Booger trying to keep his voice even. "Now, please listen carefully to what I'm going to say. I am not for sale. Neither is Winslow School. We will not sell our soul to the likes of you. Now, you and your son have a decision to make and you have two choices. He may remain here at Winslow where he will obey our rules and abide by our standards or he can pack his stuff and you can take him with you when you go. I suggest you all talk it over. He's waiting outside."

The Booger rose and opened the office door. The meeting was obviously over. Mr. Johnson walked out in a daze without saying anything.

Train stood up as his father came into the waiting area. "What's the verdict?" he asked. There was a cockiness in his voice.

Mr. Johnson grabbed him by the arm and pulled him toward the door. "We need to talk," he said.

The Booger watched the two get into Mr. Johnson's car and could tell the discussion got heated very quickly. There was a lot of arm waving and pounding on the seats and dash. He buzzed Mr. Breckenridge. "Come over here if you'd like to see some drama." He did and they sat and watched the silent production play out. After almost an hour, Train got out and slammed the car door. He walked up toward the classroom building with his head down and his hands in his pockets. Mr. Johnson remained in the car.

"Probably sending him to get his stuff, "observed Mr. Breckenridge.

"Possibly," replied The Booger.

"What was his offer?" asked Mr. Breckenridge.

"Two blank checks. One for me. One for the School. No limit."

"My, my, isn't that something."

"Sure is."

"Just think of all that money."

"It would have been a pile."

"Kinda makes you feel good to get to turn it down doesn't it, Glenn?"

"That is does, Jonas, that it does."

Mr. Breckenridge went back to his office and The Booger went back to his reports.

The buzz from the intercom startled him. "Mr. Johnson would like to speak with you," said the receptionist. A quick glance confirmed that the car had not moved. "Send him in," The Booger answered.

When Mr. Johnson came in, it was obvious he'd lost most of his bravado. He sort of slumped in the chair. The Booger waited for him to speak. "I'm sure you know that I've been sitting out in the car for a while now." The Booger nodded. "I've been doing a lot of soul searching and I've not been happy with what I've found. First of all, I want to offer you my most sincere apology. I hope you can find a way to accept it."

"It's accepted," replied The Booger.

Mr. Johnson continued. "The war made me a rich man and believe it or not I made the money honestly. But the money changed me - and not for the better. I found out just how powerful money is. Most people have a price. You can get what you want because you're rich. I've operated that way for the past few years. You folks are the first people to tell me to go to Hell in quite a while and I needed to hear it. Train will be staying. He's in your hands. Do with him whatever needs to be done. I trust your judgment. He's made a hard bed for himself by shooting off his mouth and he's going to have to rectify the situation. I'm just sorry he followed my poor example. He told me about his meeting with Coach Buck. I'm beyond embarrassed. I will apologize to that man before the school year is out when I get up enough courage to look him in the face."

Mr. Johnson stopped and wiped his face with his handkerchief. He looked wilted. "Well, I guess that's it. Thanks for hearing me out." He rose to leave.

"Thank you for coming back. It took a lot of courage," responded The Booger.

"If I could find as much courage as I've had stupidity, I'd be a hero," replied Mr. Johnson with a half-smile on his lips.

They shook hands warmly. "Here's my card. If you need me, call anytime day or night. And be sure to call collect."

* * *

About ten days after Mr. Johnson's visit, The Booger sent for Train. "How're things going?" he asked.

"Pretty well, sir, I guess. I've caught a lot of flak from some of the guys but I've just kinda kept my head down and in my books. It seems to be letting up a little."

"That's smart. Smarter than you were before."

"Yes, sir. You can say that again."

"Okay, let's talk about the first semester of biology you failed. It will have to be made up before you enroll in the fall. It can be done in a summer school we approve since we don't do a summer school here. There is probably one available where you live. However, I understand you are on a summer baseball team. How would that mesh with summer school?"

"Probably not too well, sir. I'd probably have to miss some of the out-of-town games."

"Well, that's not too good," continued The Booger. "I've been talking to Mr. Spencer. In fact, I've been talking to all your teachers. They all give you good reports. Now, Mr. Spencer is willing to give you a chance to avoid summer school. He will allow you to do a number of make-up lessons from first semester. You must perform well on all of them. There'll be no averaging.

If you start messing up on them, it's all over. In addition to these lessons, you must make a "B" this semester. If you can manage this, he will pass you for the year - no summer school."

Train's eyes lit up. "Thank you, sir, thank you."

"It's not going to be easy," warned The Booger.

"That's okay. I can do it. I'll get it done."

"Let's hope so," said The Booger. "And there's a couple of lessons I hope you have learned from all this."

"Yes, sir?"

"Number one is that it's always best to do things right the first time. And secondly, it's a good idea not to let your mouth overload your butt."

"Yes, sir. I'll remember those."

"Now, one other thing. Have you apologized to Coach Buck?"

Train dropped his head. "No, sir. I've wanted to but I'm afraid he'll mop up the floor with me."

"Well, he might. But that's the chance you're going to have to take. The ball's in your court. You're gonna have to make the move."

"Yes sir. I know."

"That's all. You're dismissed."

"Thank you, sir."

* * *

The first knock on the door was so light that Coach Buck didn't hear it. The second was louder. "Come on in."

Train opened the door a crack and slithered in like a shadow. He stood with his head down and his hands behind his back. "Well, Mr. Train Johnson," said Coach Buck. "I see you've returned to the scene of the crime."

"Yes, sir," Train replied, his words almost inaudible.

"Is there something I can do for you?"

"Yes sir, I've come to apologize."

"Who sent you?"

"Nobody."

"Nobody's making you come?"

"No sir."

"Why do you want to apologize?"

"Because I was wrong and I was disrespectful and I want to play ball again for you sometime."

As Coach Buck got to his feet, Train flinched noticeably. "Don't be scared, son. If I were going to hurt you I'd have done it the other day." Coach Buck extended his hand. "Apology accepted." Train smiled for the first time.

"There is something else, Coach."

"Okay. What is it?"

"I know I can't play this year but do the rules say anything about practice?"

"No. I think you're okay to practice."

"Then, I'd like to volunteer to be batting practice pitcher this year. It would take that load off the regular pitchers and it'd get my arm in shape for summer ball. And maybe I could help the team in some other ways also."

Coach Buck thought for a moment. "I appreciate that offer but I'm not gonna say 'yes' right now. I'll let you do it only if your grades are in good shape and stay in good shape. I'll let you know one way or the other when practice starts."

"Thank you, Coach. My grades will be up there. You're looking at your batting practice pitcher." There was a spring in Train's step as he left Coach Buck's office.

* * *

The graduation ceremony had just ended and all the caps and gone into the air. Graduates, parents, and well-wishers and all the other students were milling about talking and laughing. The Booger was standing on the edge of the crowd when he saw Train Johnson's father making his way toward him. He had a package under his arm. He gave The Booger a warm handshake. "I want to thank you and Winslow for helping my son on his way to being a man and also for helping me." There was sincerity in his voice.

"Thank you. We appreciate the compliment," responded The Booger.

"And I want to show you something," Mr. Johnson continued as he removed a picture frame from the bag. There all matted in a nice frame were the two checks The Booger had torn into pieces. They had been put back together but not so well that the jagged tears were not visible. The staple holes could also be seen. "I have these hanging on my office wall to remind me of some things I don't need to forget."

"I'm flattered," said The Booger.

"And here's something else," said Mr. Johnson handing The Booger an envelope. He opened it and pulled out a check. He looked at it and then looked again. He thought his eyes must be playing a trick on him. He tried but he couldn't speak. "Just a token of my appreciation. There are no strings on this one." Mr. Johnson disappeared into the crowd leaving The Booger looking at the check. He'd never before seen a check for a half million dollars.

The Trail

Demos sat on an empty ammo box at the makeshift table. The map was spread out but he really wasn't seeing it. His thoughts were on last night's raiding party. It was now close to noon. They should have returned hours ago. Was this another failed mission? Had they been captured or killed? What about the boy? These and other nagging questions took his mind off the map and the next mission. He rose abruptly knocking over the box seat and sweeping the map into the corner of the tent with one swipe of his hand. He threw back the flap and stomped outside.

Members of his guerrilla band sat in small groups, smoking and talking. He felt all eyes on him as he walked among the tents. He knew what they were saying. That his band was jinxed. That too many missions were failing, too many men were dying. That's why fighters were leaving his band to join others, why he was not able to recruit new men. In front of the supply tent the cook was stirring a large pot of stew. "Will you eat?" he asked. He shook his head and walked on.

It had been a simple mission: derail one of the Junta's supply trains. Four men. An isolated spot. Pull a few spikes. Drive a pre-cut timber between the rails with a sledgehammer to spread them a few inches. Be far away when the train came. A low-risk mission. A perfect one for the boy to go on. The boy was only 15. His mother had opposed his joining but he refused to listen to her pleas. He wanted to help free his country from the iron grip of the military Junta.

There could be valid reasons for their late return—but the knot in Demos' gut told him to expect the worst.

He walked along the ridgeline until he came to the rock out-cropping. He sat down on a log and looked out over the peaceful valley. It belied the political turmoil that gripped his country. He had a good view of the road.

Demos knew his band was not jinxed. It had been infiltrated. The Junta had compromised one of his men. Since he had had no new recruits for several months, it had to be one of his veterans. The agent was tricky and smart. Not every mission failed and there seemed to be no pattern to the ones that did. But he had been suspicious for some time and had been putting together bits and pieces of evidence. If last night's group had been ambushed, he would know for sure. But before he acted he had to know what had happened.

He had dealt with spies before. A quick, unexpected bullet to the head settled the matter. But there was a perverseness about this agent that called for a different action. If he'd been responsible for killing the boy, he'd lure him into walking the trail and force him to face his executioner. The first bullet would incapacitate. The others would ensure a slow and painful death.

There was a movement on the road. Demos lifted his field glasses. For a time the object was partially obscured behind leafy boughs but then it moved into an open patch. It was Demitri, a local farmer, with a wagon load of hay. He was one of the local sympathizers who provided his band with food and information. The guerrillas had the support of the people but the Junta had the army. Demitri would be bringing news.

Demos got to his feet and hurried toward the camp. The men were eating. Carlos, his second in command, rose to his feet. "Is there news?" he asked.

"Demitri is coming," Demos replied. "Bring two men." He

got his rifle from his tent and the party headed down to the road. They hid themselves in the brush, two on each side. You couldn't be too careful. Sometimes soldiers would hide in a hay wagon to pick off careless guerrillas.

As the wagon approached, one of the men walked out into the middle of the road. Demitri puled up his horses and gave the signal that all was clear. The other three came out to the wagon. Greetings were exchanged but the farmer looked straight ahead. "Well?"

He still did not alter his gaze. "They're under the hay." Demos stood rooted by the front of the wagon. The others went to the rear and began to feel under the hay. As they dragged out the bodies, Demos asked, "How many?"

"Four," Carlos answered. Demos' legs felt as if they would give way. He clutched the front wheel of the wagon for support. "An ambush?" he asked.

For the first time the farmer turned his head and looked at the rebel leader. "Yes. I'm sorry." His eyes were sad.

Demos reached up and squeezed his arm. "It's not your fault, my friend," he said. "Thank you for bringing them." Demitri nodded but did not speak.

"All out," reported Carlos from the rear. Demos stepped back. Demitri flicked the reins and the horses moved ahead.

He walked over to where the bodies had been laid out beside the road. They were grotesque in their rigor. Their open eyes stared at nothing. He felt the attack coming on. They usually came in the darkness after he'd gone to bed. He turned on his heel and headed up the hill to the camp.

The cook was cleaning up after the meal. He spoke to no one as he went straight to his tent. He threw his rifle on his cot and fell to the ground on his hands and knees as his body began to shake as it was racked by violent sobs. His tears puddled up on the canvas floor. Even in the midst of the attack, his mind raced ahead to the trail and the impending execution. He heard someone enter but saw only the boots. It had to be Carlos. He did not want to be seen this way but the tremors would not stop.

After what seemed like an eternity, the shaking and tears ceased. He straightened up, sat back on his haunches, and wiped his face on the sleeves of his shirt. "How long has this been going on?" Carlos asked.

"Since the missions started failing," answered Demos. He got to his feet, sat down on his cot, and motioned Carlos to sit on the ammo box. "They always come in the night. But this is nothing to talk about. There is work to do. Graves must be dug."

"The men are digging them now," said Carlos.

"We must send to the village for the Priest."

"That has been done."

"You think of everything, Carlos, my friend. What would I do without you?"

"We both work for The Cause," Carlos answered.

"The families must be notified."

"Messengers have been sent—except for...." Carlos' voice trailed off.

"Yes?"

"Except for the boy. I thought you would want to inform his mother."

"Yes. You are right. I will go after dark." Demos sat for several minutes with his head down lost in thought. Finally he spoke. "But now we must plan our next mission."

The words seemed to startle Carlos. "So soon?" he asked.

"Yes. The Junta must not think they can frighten us. This will be a major strike involving the whole camp."

Carlos seemed nervous. "My friend, I would counsel caution after last night's ambush."

"Caution will never topple the Junta," countered Demos as he rose to his feet, put his pistol in his holster, and picked up his rifle.

Carlos' voice took on a pleading tone. "We must not be foolhardy. And you must remember that you have just lost your son."

"All the more reason to move forward," responded Demos. He walked decisively from the tent but paused just outside as the sounds of digging came to his ears. He turned and pulled back the flap before speaking. "There is much planning to be done. Come, Carlos, my friend and walk the trail with me."

Just Another Good Day in The Park

Carl was instantly awake. All his senses were on high alert. However, to anyone observing him, no matter how closely, there was no perceptible change. Years of training had taught him to awaken this way in case there was an enemy nearby which would call for swift and decisive action. Those days were long past but old habits are hard to break. He cracked one eye lid just a fraction. No enemies were about so he stretched and listened to the sounds coming from the kitchen - Margie rattling dishes and pans, she and Nathan talking, Josh's high-pitched voice as he got ready for school. Carl would not intrude on their family time. He felt as if having him at the table each evening was enough intrusion.

He rolled out of bed, opened the blinds and looked out. About all he could see from the fifth-floor apartment was another building but he still liked to look at the world. The forecast on the 11:00 o'clock news had said "40 degrees and sunny." Not a bad day.

By the time he'd taken a shower and dressed, the kitchen was quiet. He walked down the hall to it and found Margie sitting at the table, sipping coffee, and reading the morning paper. "Morning, Pops," was her cherry greeting.

"Morning, girl." He gave her a hug and sat down.

"I made pancakes and bacon this morning."

"Sounds like a winner to me."

She got up and poured a cup of coffee. He picked up the sports section. She busied herself with the batter. "How many?"

"Oh, I think a four-stack will be plenty."

After pouring the batter on the griddle, she said, "Pops, Nathan and I have been talking."

Carl grunted. "Well, that can't be good."

"It's not bad. We just think that we don't need to continue taking your money for rent each month. You just need to use that for yourself."

Carl snorted. "Well, you're going to. You know that was our agreement. I agreed to come live with you only if I paid my own way.

"I know but we don't need the money. Nathan makes good money at the law firm and I do okay as the day hostess at the restaurant. And with your heart condition, you really don't need to live alone anymore since Mom died.

"Then just add it to Josh's college fund. And I didn't have a heart attack. The doc says those stints have me fixed up fine."

"I know, but you do so much more around here than just pay rent. You do the laundry each week; you buy a lot of the groceries; you help with Josh. We really ought to be paying you."

"That's just being family. And besides, what else would I do with the money? I'm too old to hit the bar scene every night. I'm gonna pay my way just like we agreed on."

"You know, Pops, we could just stop putting your rent checks in the bank."

"Well, you just do that and I'll take my money and go rent a cold water flat in a seedy part of town and one cold winter night when the heat breaks down, I'll die of exposure and all of your friends will say, 'That poor old man. His daughter had plenty of room but she sent him to live in the slums. Now look at what's happened.'"

"Oh, Pops, you're impossible."

"I know. But I'm lovable."

"You're also a stubborn old buzzard," she said as she sat his stack of pancakes in front of him. "I told Nathan I didn't think I'd get very far."

"And you didn't," he broke in, "but I'll tell him you gave it a good shot."

"You don't have to tell him anything. He knows you. Now, let's talk about something else. What have you got on for today?"

"Well, I'm meeting Tully down at the park this morning. We'll sit on our favorite bench and solve the world's problems. Then get home in time to get my nap in before Josh comes in from school."

"You're at the park with Tully every day in good weather. How do you find anything new to talk about?"

"We were in the Navy together. We've got plenty to talk about."

"Where's lunch going to be today?"

"We're leaning toward The Breckenridge. We hear they've got a nice hostess."

"I don't know about that. I hear she can be pretty hard on dottery old geezers."

"We're gonna try her anyway. Will she save us our special table?"

"She'll try. Are you all good tippers?"

"Tully is. I can't tip much. I've gotta pay too much rent." They both laughed.

"Another thing, Pops, isn't it a little cold to be sitting out on a park bench?"

"It's gonna be 40 degrees."

"But that's mid-afternoon. It's about 30 now."

"We'll be wrapped up. I'll wear my service coat. And if we get chilly we'll go across the street to Bennie's Diner and warm up inside with a cup of coffee. I think Tully's got the hots for that little waitress."

"Now I know you're both impossible. But there's something else that bothers me. I hear there's been some gang activity around the park. I'd hate it if you two ran into some local toughs."

Carl bristled. "Why I'll have you know..."

"Yes, I know Pops,' Margie broke in, "You're a highly trained Navy Seal and you can take care of yourself. But for Pete's sake you're 74 years old."

"Don't forget Tully. He's a Seal, too, and we're not going to let a bunch of punks keep us from using a public park in broad day light. And the doc says the fresh air is good for me and the 4-block walk to the park is also good for me.

Realizing she'd lost another round, Margie got up and cleared the table.

The air was nippy enough for Carl to pull the knit cap down over his ears but the crisp air felt good on his face. His steps were strong. He prided himself on how fit he'd kept himself over the years. He never thought his heart would play out on him. He always walked with his right hand in his coat pocket. Today it was chilly enough for both hands to be inside.

Tully was already on the bench when Carl walked up. "Did you warm up a spot for me?" Carl asked.

"Warm up your own spot. Your butt's a lot bigger than mine," Tully shot back. Both men laughed and shook hands. Carl plopped down on Tully's left. They sat engaging in good-natured banter and insults as good, long-time friends are prone to do.

After a few minutes, they realized they were not alone. About 30 yards away across a grassy area, four young men had materialized. They all wore red, billed caps with the bills over their left ear. Their athletic shoes were the same color as the caps. They stood in a circle, talking.

Every so often one would turn and look at the two old men on the bench. "Looks like we've got trouble," said Tully.

"I'd say you're right," responded Carl. They watched as the group began to engage in what looked like the "rock, paper, scissors" game. "They're choosing someone," observed Carl. Soon, three all pointed to the fourth. He'd either won or lost. He detached himself from the group and came toward the two men on the bench. He walked with a swagger. His three companions watched. The old men waited.

The boy looked to be about 18 or so. He was tall and skinny and wore a pair of jeans with frayed holes one of which framed his right knee cap. He stopped directly in front of the men. "Good morning, gentsmen, how is you two today?"

"We're good," answered Tully. Carl decided to let him speak for both of them.

"At's good. We's glad to see you both 'cause we's out dis morning making collections for our favorite charity an' we thinks you two mens would like to make a contribution."

"What might your favorite charity be?" asked Tully playing along.

"Why, you is looking at it. It's us. Jes' us four."

"How much contribution are you looking for?"

"Jes' whatever you have in your pockets." The boy paused for effect, then continued, "an' your credit cards, your watches, rings. You see we kin use mos' anything of value."

"What if we really don't want to make that large of a contribution?"

"Well, 'den we calls on Mr. Collector to help change yo' mind." As the boy spoke, his right hand slithered out of his jacket pocket and the switchblade opened with a sinister sound. The blade was wide and about nine inches long and appeared to be honed to a razor edge.

The two-man looked at each other. Tully's eyes asked, "Now?"

Carl's short nod from side to side said, "Not yet."

"I'll have to get up to get my billfold," said Carl as he began to rock to get up like many old people. However, on his second rock, he raised his right leg a little higher and as he came forward, he slid to the edge of the bench and his leg shot forward with tremendous force aimed at the exposed kneecap. As the heavy boot sole hit the target, Carl could feel the ligaments snap and the knee joint fold backward. The boy dropped the knife as he went down and lay on the ground screaming and writhing in pain. His three companions began to run toward them with similar knives in their hands.

"I guess it's time now," said Tully.

"I'd say so," responded Carl.

The two men pulled their right hands from their coats. Their three attackers skidded to a stop. Their mouths gaped open and their eyes were wide with fear. They were looking down the barrels of two military .45 caliber automatics in the hands of two old guys who looked as if they knew how to use them. The boy on the ground was quiet, having passed out from the pain.

Tully spoke. "Get on your knees, boys." They did so. "Pitch

your knives right over there." He pointed and they did so. "You know, Carl, I think we oughta just kill all of 'em." One began to sob. The other two began to beg.

"You really think so?" asked Carl.

"Sure do. There's just two apiece. That's no big deal. We've done in a lot more'n this several times."

"Please mister, don't kill us," one begged. "We'll leave and won't ever come back or bother you no more." The front of the pants of the boy who was crying began to turn wet and dark as he lost control of his bladder.

"Do you think the city would give us a medal if we killed 'em all?" asked Carl. The two begged harder. The crier peed more

"Probably," observed Tully. "Let's get 'em on the ground while we decide. Okay, boys, face down on the ground. Arms stretched out in front." The attackers rushed to comply.

Carl took out his cell and dialed 911. People who'd heard the first screams began to show up. Soon sirens could be heard and flashing lights on police cars and ambulances could be seen at the park entrance. The police and a large crowd seemed to get there at the same time. There was a local TV crew in the mix. The boy on the ground with the funny looking leg came to and began to scream again. The police and medics took over and got things under control They loaded everybody up and hauled one to the hospital and the rest down to the station where they booked the culprits and took statements from Carl and Tully. The police let them keep the guns since they both had carry permits and since they'd not shot anybody with them. As they were taking them back home in a squad car, Tully observed, "Most excitement I've had in a long time. Nice to know we can still function."

"It is, partner, it sure is," agreed Carl.

Carl asked the officer to drop them off down the street from The Breckenridge. It wouldn't do for Margie to see them getting out of a squad car. As they walked in, Margie asked, "Two gentlemen for lunch?"

"That's right," answered Tully, "is our favorite table open?"

"It most certainly is. Have you gents had a good morning?"

"Yes," answered Carl winking at Tully, "just another good day in the park."

The Device

Woody opened one eye and looked at the clock on the bedside table. It read 8:06, about the time he usually woke up. Out of habit he stretched an arm out to the other side of the bed even though he knew what he wouldn't find. The sheets were cool and the space empty. Jenny had been dead a little more than a year now but it still seemed as if she should be there. The house was quiet. He reached over to the control box beside the clock and turned off the alarm system which consisted of motion detectors throughout the house. He threw back the covers and swung his legs out to sit on the side of the bed while sliding his hand under his pillow and bringing out the pistol which he placed in the drawer of the bedside table. His philosophy was always to have a little back up just in case.

He went to the window and looked out although he did not open the blinds but went to one side and spread two slats slightly and peered through. All seemed normal. He went to the bathroom and emptied his bladder and splashed some cold water on his face before going down the hall to his workout room. He liked to do a few reps first thing every morning just to get his body loose. A longer workout would follow later in the day. These daily exercises made him feel good and also were the reason his body looked twenty years younger than his 74 years. As he picked up the hand weight, a sharp pain shot through his right hand, bringing into focus the incident of yesterday afternoon. He released his grip on the piece of equipment and sat down on a weight bench to examine his hand. It was swollen some but all the fingers seemed to be functioning. There didn't appear to be a break. Nothing was out of place. One of the metacarpal bones could be cracked but it would take an x-ray to show that. If it didn't improve in due time he'd see about it. He just sat dejectedly with his forearms on his thighs and his head down, trying to figure out how he'd let himself mess up so badly.

He'd managed to fly under the radar for almost 25 years - always looking over his shoulder and never causing a ripple in the water. Even when Jenny died, he'd gotten her cremated without fanfare. Could his new interest in coins be to blame? It gave him something to do and he had avoided falling into any pattern with it. He was currently working on quarters. He'd get ten rolls at a bank and look at each coin under his scope. Occasionally, he'd run across an old, valuable one but mostly he'd find those with some flaw that set them apart. These would go to his collection, the coins would be re-rolled, and traded for another ten rolls. And he always went to a different branch to do the swap. With the number of branches in town, he wouldn't be in the same one even twice in two years. No pattern there. And when he went to places where he knew there were security cameras, he always wore a nondescript hat or cap with no logo and dark glasses. His shirts or jackets were equally plain. No, there didn't seem to be any way to predict that his and that idiot's paths would cross.

It was late afternoon. He had gone to a small branch across town to swap his quarters. There were two teller stations open with a couple of customers waiting at each one. He chose the one on the right and stood behind a young woman in a short dress with nice legs and a jiggly butt. Might as well have something nice to look at while he waited. As the woman was completing her transaction, he took a roll of quarters out of his little canvas sack to start the swapping. But then a person materialized on his left and a voice said, "Just move over, pops, and you won't get hurt." He turned to see the man pull an automatic from under his jacket and moved to the right as he'd been told to do. Realizing something was going on behind her, the woman turned around and looked down the barrel of the pistol. Her eyes widened and she sucked in a large gulp of air in preparation for a scream. "Make a sound and you're dead," the robber hissed at her. She stifled the scream and began to whimper. "Move it that way," he directed motioning to the left. She did. Pitching a folded canvas bag to the teller, he ordered, "Fill it up.

And no dye packs or you're dead." Then he spoke to the frightened customer, "I think I'll just take you with me You'd be good insurance." The woman looked ready to collapse.

As the teller filled the bag, Woody studied the man. He had a wild look in his eyes, a flushed face, and was so nervous he couldn't hold the gun steady. He was high on something and was likely to start shooting at the slightest provocation. The teller had probably hit the silent alarm but if he started out of the bank with that woman as a hostage, all hell would break loose. What Woody needed was an opening. His fist clinched around the roll of quarters and his muscles tensed like a coiled spring. Finally, the robber dropped the muzzle of the gun so that it pointed down at the marble counter front. The pent-up energy in Woody's muscles exploded. His quarter-loaded fist caught the robber just under his right cheek bone. Woody felt bones break. Blood along with several teeth flew out and onto the teller. The gun went off but the bullet only knocked a chip out of the marble and ricocheted down into the carpet. The gun dropped to the floor. The robber fell into the woman and they both went down in a pile. She began to scream and fight to get free of the now unconscious bandit who was bleeding all over her. People came running from all directions. Woody backed away, and in all the confusion, slipped out the door with his quarters and disappeared.

Why did he take such a chance? He didn't care about the bank's money. That was no skin off his butt. He didn't want to admit it at first but it was the young woman - and the other innocent people that doped up screwball was on the verge of shooting. A few years ago they wouldn't have mattered to him any more than the bank's money did today. "I must be getting soft in my old age," Woody thought to himself.

He went downstairs and started the coffee maker. He went to the windows on all sides of the house and peeked through the blinds as he had done upstairs. Nothing seemed out of place. He slipped a gun into the pocket of his robe, went through the garage, and a side door, and down the curved driveway to pick up his morning paper. The place was perfect for him - near the city, rugged terrain, not many houses, no close neighbors, a place to be let alone. Re-entering the house, he poured a cup of coffee, sat down at the kitchen table, and slipped the paper out of its plastic sleeve. As he opened it and saw the picture, he almost dropped his coffee cup. It was a large picture of him taken by the bank's security camera. The bold headline, a take-off on the closing line of a Lone Ranger episode, read, "Who was that (un)masked man?"

After he regained his composure, he read the story. Folks at the bank said they'd never seen the old fellow before. They estimated his age at about 60. Woody was flattered. The story went on quoting the doctors at the hospital saying that they'd never seen so much damage from one blow by a fist. Practically all the bones including the eye socket on one side of his face were broken and would require extensive reconstruction. They'd also had a hard time treating him because of all the drugs in his system. Woody had been right on all counts. The bank was also offering a $5,000 reward for thwarting the robbery if the gentleman would come forward. "Don't hold your breath on that," Woody thought to himself.

He examined the photo closely. It was grainy and a little out of focus. Maybe no one would recognize him. The age 60 estimation was in his favor. He debated about calling Clarence but finally decided to see if he could ride it out. If he were not identified quickly, maybe things would die down.

The rest of the morning was spent puttering around the house. He ate an early lunch and then tied up the cap, shirt, and sunglasses he'd had on yesterday in a trash bag before heading for work at Draper's Appliance and Electrical Supply. On the way he drove behind a large strip mall and threw the bag into a dumpster. He'd worked at Draper's in the repair division for over 20 years. Back in the shop he didn't have to deal with the public. It was a perfect place to work and hide. He was semi-retired now. Only worked afternoons and he could name which ones. He was so good with anything electrical that they were just glad to have him anytime he wanted to work.

He had just gotten to his work area and was looking over the repair orders when Charlie, the shop foreman, came up. "Is that your picture in the paper?" he asked.

Woody played dumb. "What picture? I haven't done anything to get a picture in the paper."

"This picture," answered Charlie as he plopped the paper down on the table. Woody did a double take. "There's your white mustache and your white hair showing around your cap."

Woody pretended to look at the picture more closely. "Well, it does sorta look like me. What'd this fellow do?"

"Thwarted a bank robbery."

"Are you serious?" Woody picked up the paper and started to "read" the article. "Why this happened at a Planter's National branch up north of town. I don't ever go up that direction. I bank at the Citizen's Bank and Trust just down the street here." Woody continued to "read." "And it says here he's about 60. Shoot, I'm 74. But, you know, he sure does look a lot like me." He handed the paper back.

"I was hoping we had a celebrity on our hands," said Charlie.

"Sorry about that. But do you think I ought to go up and apply for that reward? We could split it," Woody joked.

"Probably not. But it's a thought." Charlie picked up the paper and started to leave. "Jackie's got two vacuum cleaners he can't get right. See what he needs to do."

"Be glad to," answered Woody.

As Charlie headed back to his little office, Woody heard him tell one of the other technicians, "Nah, that's not him." Woody breathed a sigh of relief. So far, so good.

On the way home, he picked up some Chinese and sat down to eat and watch Brian Williams and NBC's evening news. He almost choked when his picture flashed on the screen. The story had gone national. He dreaded it. He wished Norman had not retired. He had been more understanding. Clarence was one of the "new breed." Didn't have much respect or appreciation for the older ones in the program. He turned the TV off, picked up his cell, and dialed Clarence's number. He answered after the second ring. This is Woody."

"Woody who?" Woody knew Clarence had caller ID and

knew who was calling but he was going to make him go through the whole code thing.

"Woody Woodenhoffer."

"Where do you live?"

"In the woods on the beach."

"Who do you live with?"

"Two chipmonks and a ground hog."

"What are their names?"

"Chip and Dale and Pauxatawny Phil."

"We've been wondering if you were going to call. We thought maybe you'd let us know something after you went on Letterman and Larry King."

"Very funny. I'm gonna need to be moved."

"Moved? Just like that? You go and get yourself on national news and then just snap your fingers and expect us to take care of you?"

"That was the agreement."

"That's right, my friend, but you agreed to keep your head down and do nothing to call attention to yourself. And that's sure not the case here. I'm getting tired of fooling with you damned criminals."

"Listen, if I hadn't hit that guy, there's no telling how many people would have gotten shot. And the Bureau didn't seem to mind for some of us 'criminals' to help them put away a lot of the Mob 25 years ago."

"Well, that was 25 years ago. Times have changed. The Mob has probably forgotten about you by now."

"Don't give me that. You know the Mob never forgets. I tell you, I need to be moved." Woody's tone was becoming more urgent.

"Maybe you ought to read the papers. Every department's under budget constraints. We don't have the money to be moving a lotta you old crooks around when you get skiddish or when you screw up like you just did."

"What if I just move on my own?"

"If you do, you'll be out of the witness protection program and totally on your own."

"What the hell am I supposed to do then?"

"Well, you've changed a lot. Your hair's white. You've got a mustache. We're gonna gamble that they won't recognize you."

"You know it's my life you're gambling with. You don't have a hell of a lot to lose."

"You're right. But if the Mob does show up, you call me and we'll move you anywhere in the country you want to go - no questions asked."

"That's real big of you." There was sarcasm in Woody's voice. "And how am I gonna know they're here before they start shooting? Maybe I won't die immediately and can punch your number in as I draw my last breath."

"Surely you learned something in all your years with the Mob. Survival should have been one of those things. If they find you, use some of those skills to stay alive. Then we'll take care of you."

Woody was so angry that he could hardly speak. "Okay, you ass hole, I'm gonna stay alive just to spite you. But I'm warning you, it may not be pretty."

"I don't care about pretty. I'm just interested in the bottom line."

Woody pushed the "off" button without saying "goodbye." He began to bang his fist on the table in frustration but it hurt so bad he had to stop. He sat back in his chair and waited for the wave of anger to subside. Acting out of anger would not be prudent. If he were going to survive, he'd have to be cold and calculating. Slowly, his body relaxed and he sat for almost an hour in deep thought. Gradually, a plan began to emerge.

He went into the bathroom and stood looking at himself in the mirror. He had a full head of white hair and a white mustache. He'd grow a full beard and then dye it and his hair. That would change his appearance a good bit. And he didn't need a house. He'd go to one of those retirement communities out West and get a small condo. People were always moving in and out from all over the country. He'd hardly be noticed.

Next, he began to get items together to take with him. These he stacked on the dining room table. He went out to his workshop in one corner of the garage and checked his supplies. He made a list of what he'd need to make a "device." He had sworn never to make another one when he left the Mob but this was a matter of survival. He didn't know how he might use it or even if he would use it but he'd have it just in case. What he didn't have was available from work - everything except the core material. That would take a little doing but he felt sure he could swing it.

Woody wondered just how the Mob would "take care of him." They might hire a professional hit man who'd use a sniper rifle from a distance or a gun with a silencer up close. If that were the case, he wouldn't stand much of a chance. On the other hand, his was an old situation and the new Mob leadership wouldn't have a personal interest. Woody was going to gamble that they'd take care of things "in house" and send a couple of goons to do the job. Woody thought he'd be able to deal with that scenario.

The next few days were especially hectic and stressful. He gassed up his van, backed it into the garage, and started packing it. Jenny's car became his transportation. Several mornings were spent securing the type of explosive he'd need. Evenings were spent on the internet researching retirement communities in the West and in his shop building the device. He went nowhere, even to the bathroom, without being armed. No longer did he walk down to pick up the paper or to the mailbox. These chores were done quickly from the car with a wary eye on any approaching vehicle. He altered the time he left for work and never drove the same route. He parked in a different place every day and walked a zig-zag pattern between parked cars using the larger ones for cover. He put a mirror over his work bench so that he could see anyone approaching. He looked at every person, every car, and every area with suspicion, hoping to pick up any clue that would give him an edge.

Within ten days he was ready. The van was packed. The device was made. Each night he placed it in a flower box by his front door in case the hit man came posing as a magazine salesman and rang the doorbell. All the blinds and drapes were kept closed night and day. No lights were turned on at night. The garage doors were in the back so the only discernable activity was his car going in or out the driveway. Otherwise the house appeared deserted.

Now the waiting - the nerve-wracking waiting - began. He became jumpy and reacted to any loud noise or sudden movement. Charlie noticed and asked him about it. He passed it off saying he just wasn't sleeping well - which was the truth. A week went by. Nothing. He'd go to the front window two or three times a day and survey the strip mall's parking lot looking for anything out of place. Everything was always normal.

Then one afternoon a few minutes before closing time, he saw something out of place. Backed into a slot on the far side of the lot was a large, black sedan. It was facing the store and had no other cars near it. All the windows were dark so that you couldn't see in but the front seat windows were down about three inches allowing tobacco smoke to escape. Yes, the Mob had sent two goons. If they'd been smart, they'd have parked in with other cars and not been advertising their presence by sending up smoke signals. He found Ernie, the store's errand boy, gave him his keys, and asked him to bring his car around to the delivery entrance at the rear. From there he could get out onto a side street without being seen from the parking lot. He was hoping they did not know where he lived.

He went straight home and didn't even stop to get the mail from the mail box. He shut the garage door behind him, raced in and got his computer, and put it into the van. He ran upstairs and threw a few personal items into a canvas bag. He went to a front window which gave a good view of the road and peeked through the blinds. Everything looked clear but then his heart jumped up in his throat as the black car came slowly cruising by. It went down a ways turned around, and came back. This time it stopped at his mail box, the window went down, and the person opened and closed the box. Woody was glad he'd left his mail. The car went on down the road, turned around, and came back and parked on the side of the road about a hundred yards from the driveway. He was trapped.

For a few minutes, his mind simply would not focus. He paced the floor with his mind throwing out all manner of panicked thoughts none of which fit together. Finally, he sat down and made himself think rationally. First of all, they were unaware he'd made them. They thought he was not home yet.

He doubted they wanted to come into his house. They were waiting to catch him outside probably as he stopped at the mail box. He could take them by surprise and race down the driveway and be gone in the opposite direction before they could react. But his loaded van would be no match for their muscle car. He rejected that idea.

It would be dark soon. That was another mark in his favor. And they were just going to sit and wait. He knew where they were but they had no idea where he was. Yep, they were sitting ducks. He changed into a pair of camouflage coveralls and pulled a dark knit cap down over his white hair. He took the devise to his workshop and attached a couple of wires before slipping out the back door. He went into the woods behind his house and cut down to the road where it curved around the hill out of the sight of the parked car. There was not much shoulder and the car was parked right against the roadside bushes. He slipped through the brush until he was right at the car's right rear fender. Both windows were down a little and the two hit men were still smoking. He could hear them talking. He dropped to his knees and was preparing to slide under the car when the driver's side door popped open. He froze. Surely they hadn't heard him The man in the passenger seat spoke. "Where the hell are you going?"

"I gotta piss."

"You'd better hope he don't show up while you're doing it."

"It won't take me long," the driver said as he came around the rear of the car and began to wet down the bushes not three feet from where Woody was kneeling. Woody hunched over hiding his hands and face and trying to look like a stump. He wondered what the man had been eating. His urine had an odor that would take your breath away.

The passenger let his window all the way down. "Where the hell you think he is?"

"Probably went somewhere to eat and run an errand or two. He's gotta come home sooner or later. When he stops to get his mail, I'll pin him in and you work him over with that AK-47. We couldn't find a better spot. It's so isolated. We'll be gone before anybody sees us."

"Well, I wish he'd hurry up. I'm getting hungry. I don't shoot as well on an empty stomach."

The driver finished and returned to his seat saying, "With as many rounds as you got in that piece, you don't have to shoot well." The passenger window went back up.

Woody slid under the side of the car and up toward its front. He attached the device right beneath the front seat and slipped out the way he had come.

He threw the coveralls into a corner of the garage and put his traveling clothes on. He got into the van, took out his cell phone, and dialed the number. He pushed "send" and listened for the first ring. As the ring started the explosion came. It lit up the night and shook the house. He punched open the garage door and drove down to the street. The burning car was lying upside down crossways in the road. Various parts of it were scatter about, some up in the trees. Woody supposed he could have used a little less of a charge - but then, the Mob deserved his best shot. As he turned the opposite direction headed for a new life, he took out his cell and dialed Clarence's number.

Out of Step

The only sound came from the pendulum of the Regulator clock on the wall by the door. The old man glanced up and noted that he did not have enough time to read further, so he placed his leather bookmark at the beginning of Chapter 20 of Kathryn Stockett's The Help and closed the book. He sat back and reflected on just how far Skeeter, Stockett's main character, had been out of step with the vast majority of white Mississippians in the early 1960s. He could not keep his mind from jumping two decades earlier to a similar situation in his own small Mississippi hometown.

It was the fall of 1946 and he had just gotten his first Saturday job at the Kroger store on the square. It was a good job for a 9th grader—good spending money. Most stores and service stations paid $5.00 for a 15-hour Saturday. Kroger paid $7.00. Yes, a very good job.

The store was a service store. Customers came in with their lists and read off their items one by one to him. He'd fetch the items and stack them on the counter. After all were gathered, he'd jot down the price of each on a note pad, wait his turn at the lone cash register, ring up the order, collect the money, bag the groceries, and carry them to the car if help was needed. He'd heard of the new super markets where customers were allowed to select their own items but he'd never seen one.

Saturday was a big day in town. Most people, both white and colored, came in from the surrounding farms to shop and visit. Many would buy their groceries during the day and have the store hold them until they got ready to go home. Kroger had an empty floor space near the front door for this purpose. On Saturdays it was always filled with tall, brown paper bags with names written on the sides with a grease pencil.

About 8:00 o'clock one November Saturday evening, an elderly colored woman came in to get her groceries she'd left a few hours earlier. He located her two bags and went to the storeroom to find Webb. Webb was a colored man who was the store's Saturday handyman. One of his duties was to carry bags for colored customers. The manager had made something very clear on the boy's first Saturday. "You never carry a sack for a nigger," he'd said. That was Webb's job but he was nowhere to be found. Webb had a habit of carrying a bag and then stopping to visit a while on his way back to the store. He was probably somewhere in the throng on the square.

When he told the woman there was no one to carry her bags, she became distraught, wringing her hands and talking out loud to herself. "What's I gwine do? I cain leave my groceries. My ride is leaving. I cain walk home. I lives too fer out in de country. What is I gwine do?"

As he stood there he didn't see an old, colored woman—only a person who needed help. He looked around the store. No one was paying any attention to them. The other clerks were all busy with customers. He picked up one of her sacks and asked, "Where's the car?"

"Cross de square by de park," she answered. But then her eyes widened and a look of fear came over her face. "But you cain take my sacks...."

He cut her off. "Just walk out the door and don't look back," he directed. As she did so, he hoisted the remaining bag to his other hip and followed. He stayed about thirty feet behind her.

To the casual observer, he was only a Saturday clerk with someone's groceries. He hoped his manager didn't find out. He knew he'd be fired because the store couldn't afford to have any "nigger loving" clerks. It would cost them white business. The journey across the square was uneventful.

When they got to the park, the woman hurried ahead and spoke to a colored fellow who opened the trunk of a nearby car. There were a lot of colored people in this area, standing around, leaning on cars, talking, visiting. When they saw the white boy carrying the groceries, all activity creased. They stared at a sight they'd never seen before.

He placed the sacks in the trunk and turned to leave. The woman was thanking him over and over. She dug a little snap-open coin purse from her pocket and popped it open. "Here, mista, lets me give you a little something for your trouble." He'd carried a lot of sacks for white people but no one had ever offered to tip him.

"No, ma'am," he declined. "We don't charge anything for carrying groceries." She thanked him several more times before he got out of earshot. None of the onlookers spoke.

As he headed back across the square, he realized for the first time just how far out of step he was with most every white person he knew. A cool wind blew on his face. It felt good. And for the first time, he felt that odd sensation somewhere deep down inside—the one he would feel often during his life. It felt good, too.

A light rap on his door brought the old man back to the present. And his secretary's voice, "Five minutes, Your Honor." He rose and donned his back robe. As he strode down the hall to his courtroom, he reflected on his long, out-of-step legal career in civil rights litigation. The cool air from an air conditioning vent played across his face taking him back to that November day so long ago. The now familiar sensation welled up inside. They both still felt good.

The Surprise

"No one is so brave that he is not
disturbed by something unexpected."
--Julius Caesar

January - February 1947 at The Winslow School

It was Sunday afternoon. Mid-term exams had been finished
on Friday and everyone had enjoyed a free weekend - no
homework, no Saturday detention. Of course, Lance had
basketball practice but mostly it was a good time for the students
to rest a little before the second semester began on Monday.
Lance and Tex were just lazing around their room listening to the
radio. It was too cold to do much outside.

Suddenly, their relaxation was interrupted by a racket down
the hall. Lance stuck his head out the door and saw a strange boy
struggling with a large trunk. "Come on, Tex," he commanded as
he started down the hall. "Somebody needs some help." They
helped the fellow move the trunk and the suitcases from the
lobby into the vacant room. "I guess you're here to start the
second term," said Lance.

"That's right," the boy replied as he stuck out his hand, "I'm
Curtis Holden." Introductions were made and the three shook
hands.

"Where are you from?" asked Tex.

"Washington, D. C."

"If you don't mind my asking," said Tex, "Why didn't you
come in the fall?"

"No, I don't mind," Curtis replied. "It's kinda complicated.

My father's with the Foreign Service. You know that's the diplomats and all their staff. Anyway, we thought we'd be in Washington for a while but my dad got a new assignment to France. He didn't want to take me because they're still not back on their feet after the war, especially with the schools. There's just the two of us now since my mom died with cancer last year. My dad graduated from Winslow and most of his family still lives in Nashville which will be close for me to go during holidays. So he made some phone calls and here I am."

"Have you lived in other countries?" Lance asked.

"Oh, yes. I was born in Mexico and then we were in Brazil and Japan before the war."

"You've really been around," observed Lance. "Do you play any sports?"

"Yes. I play half back in football and short stop in base ball."

"I hope you'll come out for our teams," encouraged Lance. "We've got a great coach."

"We sure do," echoed Tex.

"I'll sure plan on it," said Curtis.

"Well, we'll go on and let you get unpacked," said Lance. "Supper is at six. If you need help with anything, just let us know."

As they went back down the hall, Lance remarked, "Seems like a nice enough fellow."

"Yes, he does," responded Tex.

***

The semester was only about two weeks old. Lance was standing at his locker getting books for his next class when he heard a loud yell and the sound of books hitting the floor. Turning around he saw Curtis Holden sprawled out in the middle of the hall with his books scattered about. Butch Bledsoe was standing over him. As Lance went over to help him pick up his stuff, he heard Butch saying, "How do you like that you damned Yankee? You shoulda stayed up North where you belong." Some of Bledsoe's cronies were standing around laughing. And as Lance was gathering up some papers, Butch addressed him, "Well if it ain't Mississippi Boy. I didn't know you were a Yankee lover."

Lance stood up abruptly and shoved Butch up against the wall. "You want me to take your sorry ass to the woods?"

"Naw. I got no beef with you," Butch answered.

"Well, you're gonna have if you don't shut your stupid mouth," threatened Lance as he helped Curtis gather up the rest of his things. Mr. Wilcox came down the hall and dispersed the crowd that had formed.

Lance told Tex about the incident and after supper they went down to Curtis' room. He was sitting at his desk reading from his Lit book. "What's the problem with you and Bledsoe?" asked Lance.

"I have no idea. I guess he just doesn't like northern people. He started in on me about the second day I was here."

"What's he been doing?" asked Tex.

"Well, mostly it's just insults, calling me names, jostling me in the hall. One day he hid my Latin book and I didn't have it for class and Mr. Benedetti jumped all over me. Of course, he tripped me today in the hall. You saw what happened there."

Tex started for the door. "I think I'll go find him right now and kick his ass."

"No. Don't do that," said Curtis. "This is my problem and I'm gonna have to deal with it. He keeps trying to get me to go to the woods with him and fight but I don't want to hurt him."

Tex and Lance exchanged books. Butch Bledsoe was much bigger than Curtis, probably outweighed him by fifty pounds and "he didn't want to hurt him?" "Well, just let us know if you need any help with anything," said Lance.

"Yeah," Tex chimed in, "I'd like to slap the shit outta Bledsoe plus all those jokers that hang around with him."

"I appreciate the offer," said Curtis, "but I'll take care of things when the time comes."

As they were on the way back to their room, Tex asked, "Did I hear right? Did he say he didn't want to hurt him?"

"That's what I heard."

"My gosh. I'd think Bledsoe would stomp him in the ground. Does he know something we don't?"

"He might, "replied Lance, "you remember what Par did to you that time in the woods."

"I sure do. And I hope Curtis has some weapons like Par did because you know as well as I do that Butch is gonna push him into a fight sooner or later."

"I'm afraid you're right, Roomie, I'm afraid you're right."

The harassment continued unabated. One day Butch shoved Curtis in t he hall. "Why don't you just leave me alone?" he asked in exasperation.

"I will when you go to the woods with me," Butch shot back. Curtis shook his head. "That's 'cause you're nothing but a yellow-bellied Yankee just like all those other Yankees." As if on cue, Butch's followers began to point at Curtis and chant "yellow belly, yellow belly, yellow belly." Curtis turned and walked away. From then on any time he passed Butch or any of his buddies he heard "yellow belly, yellow belly."

One afternoon after classes Curtis stopped by Mr. Culpepper's room to clear up questions, he had about the new algebra unit they'd begun that day. When he was done, most everybody had left the classroom building. He noticed two of Butch's gang hanging out at the other end of the hall but didn't think anything about it. As he left the building, they fell in behind at a respectable distance. Just past the library the sidewalk curved into almost a tunnel of thick evergreens. Suddenly, Butch Bledsoe and two of his buddies emerged from the thick growth, blocking his path. He turned around only to be faced by the two who were following him. He was trapped.

Butch spoke, "Since you're too chicken-livered to go the woods, we're gonna use these woods."

"This is on campus. You know we're not supposed to fight on campus."

"I know but I'm gonna make an exception in this case."

"We're not supposed to have any witnesses either."

"I'm making another exception. I just want these boys to see what a big piece of yellow Yankee chicken shit you are."

"Well, I guess I don't have much choice," said Curtis as he put his books down on the edge of the sidewalk.

"No, you don't," sneered Butch.

Curtis began to remove his shoes. "Why are you taking off ...."

Butch never got to finish the sentence. Curtis' arms snapped up in front of his face. His palms were open, a loud "EEEEE-YYYYY" came from his mouth. Suddenly, there was a flurry of chops and kicks almost too fast for the eye to see. Within five seconds Butch Bledsoe was in a bloody pile on the sidewalk. He was bleeding from the nose and mouth and both bruised eyes were rapidly swelling shut. A low moan gurgled from his throat.

His four friends stood slack-jawed in disbelief. Curtis began to slip his shoes back on and then stopped. "I'm going over and report this to Mr. Montague. Any of you want to try and stop me?" They all shook their heads and got well to one side to let Curtis pass. Then they scraped their leader off the sidewalk and helped him toward the infirmary.

The secretary buzzed The Booger and sent Curtis back to his office. "Come in, my boy," greeted the Booger cordially. "I trust you're settling in well here at Winslow. What can I do for you?"

"Well, no sir, I haven't been doing too well. I came to report a fight."

The Booger looked surprised. "Were you a participant in it?"

"Yes sir."

"Well, you don't look any the worse for it. Sit down and tell me about it."

Curtis told The Booger the whole story - about the constant harassment, the threats, how he got trapped between the bushes, and the end result. He said he didn't know the names of the other four boys.

"You say you know martial arts?"

"Yes, sir. I began taking lessons when we lived in Japan and I continued in Washington."

"You think Mr. Bledsoe went to the infirmary?"

"I expect he did, sir. I cut him up pretty good. We're not suppose to use it to hurt people but I didn't see any way out."

"If what you've told me is correct, I'd say you're right," said The Booger as he picked up the phone and dialed the infirmary. "Hello . . . yes, this is Mr. Montague. Would you please ask Nurse Hessie to come to the phone? . . . Oh, she's with a patient. Well, tell her if he's not about to die, I need to speak with her. . .

Yes, Mrs. Hessie, has a Mr. James Bledsoe been by to see you this afternoon. . . Oh, you're working on him now. How bad is he hurt. . . That bad, eh. . . I see. . . Do you think it's broken? . . .Can you patch him up or do we need to send him to Sandersville? . . . I see . . . Okay . . . Well, please give him this message for me when you get him back together. Tell him that I want to see him in my office immediately after Chapel in the morning. And he's to bring his four friends with him. I don't know who they are and I'm not going to waste time hunting them down, but he knows and they all better be here. . . Yes. . Thank you, Mrs. Hessie. Goodbye."

The Booger hung up the phone and turned to Curtis. "Anyone else know about this harassment?"

"Yes sir. Lance and Tex do. Lance has even seen some of it. Am I in trouble, sir?"

"Not if your story checks out. I appreciate your coming to report this. Just go on about your business. I'll send for you if I need you.

"Thank you sir."

After Curtis made his departure, The Booger buzzed his secretary. "Please find a boy and send him to search our Mr. Al Highsmith and ask him to come over here immediately." In a few minutes, Tex hustled in all out of breath. Their talk lasted about fifteen minutes.

The Booger knew that Lance was at basketball practice so he walked over to the gym. They were working on some defensive set-ups. He asked Coach Buck if he could see Lance for a minute. They sat down on the bleachers and talked for a time. The Booger then sat and watched a few minutes of practice before heading back to his office.

By supper time word had spread all over campus about the incident and Bledsoe's bruised face gave ample evidence of it. Lance and Tex went by Curtis' room after supper. There were two or three boys in the hall outside his door and several more inside. "Are you having a special meeting?" asked Lance as he went in.

"No," replied Curtis looking rather sheepish, "But a lot of guys are coming to congratulate me for some reason."

A boy sitting on the end of the bed spoke up. The ¬reason is that Butch Bledsoe has pissed off a lot of people."

Lance and Tex both laughed. "Well, let us in on the congratulations," said Tex as he extended his hand. They both shook Curtis' hand and then left to make room for others who were crowding in. As they walked down the hall, Tex said, "I wonder how many boys are down at Butch's room?"

"Oh, I imagine a few are going by just to get a look at his black eyes," replied Lance. Both boys laughed.

When The Booger got to his office after Chapel, the five boys were in the lobby waiting for him. Butch had on dark glasses. "I appreciate you boys taking time out of your busy schedules to see me," he said. The boys seemed to miss his sarcasm. "Come on in my office and let's take care of things." The Booger had set up five chairs in front of his desk for them. "Have you gone Hollywood on us with the sunglasses?" he asked.

"No sir. The light hurts my eyes," Butch answered.

"let me see what's behind them," The Booger commanded. As Butch removed the glasses, he winced noticeably. The Booger examined him for several seconds. "How does any light get in? I don't believe I've seen two better looking shiners."

"Not much does, sir, but even a little bit hurts."

"Okay, put 'em back on," ordered The Booger as he took out a yellow legal pad and began writing. "Mr. Bledsoe, I'm putting you at the top of my list. Now, let me get the rest of you boys on it." He called out their names as he wrote them down, "Mr. Samuel Simpkins, Mr. George Logan, Mr. Jerry Thorn, Mr. John Pitts." He continued, "I don't intend to spend a lot time on this. I'm going to tell you boys what I've found out. If I'm wrong on anything, just stop me. Understand?"

"Yes sir," they all responded.

"Mr. Bledsoe, you have been harassing Mr. Holden ever since he got here. . . You've been pushing him, tripping him, and doing any number of other things physically . . . You have been insulting him, challenging him to fight, hiding his books, and doing Lord knows what else along these lines . . . You and your buddies here trapped him yesterday on the sidewalk over near the Library and forced him to fight. . . He then proceeded to beat the ever living crap out of you." The Booger had paused after each statement and had gotten no challenges. "Could you please tell me why."

Butch spoke up. "He's a Yankee, sir."

"How can you be so stupid, son?" The Booger retorted. His grandparents live in Nashville. All his family are from the South. He just has to live where his father's profession takes him. It's this type of dumb, ill-informed, ignorant prejudice that causes so much trouble in our world and I will not condone it on this campus. Do you understand me?"

"Yes sir."

"Now, do you knuckleheads realize that with all this harassment and forcing a fight on campus with witnesses that you have committed a serious breach of Winslow's conduct code, one for which the whole lot of you could be expelled?"

The "yes sirs" came in unison.

"And look at you, Mr. Bledsoe. I taught your daddy. I'm extremely disappointed in you. How do you think he's gonna feel?"

"The same way, sir."

"And what do you think he's gonna do?"

"Well, since Curtis has about taken care of my face, I think he'll probably come up here and wear my butt out with his belt."

"Which you deserve."

"Yes, sir."

"I can tell you boys one thing for sure. I will not tolerate bullying. I will not tolerate this type of prejudicial attitude toward any segment of our student body - our northern boys, our Jewish boys, or anybody else. If you're not gonna change that, I'm gonna get rid of the whole bunch of you before you infect some of the other boys. Now, do you have anything to say for your selves?"

Butch Bledsoe spoke first. "I'd just ask that you let me apologize to Curtis before you put me on the train."

"We'd all like to do that," said Jerry Thorn.

"We've been talking," said George Logan, "and we all like Yankees a lot better than we did yesterday."

"We'd like to stay," said John Pitts.

"If you'll just let us stay, we'll do anything you say - take any punishment," said Samuel Simpkins.

A couple of the boys were wiping tears from their cheeks. The Booger looked from boy to boy with an intense gaze. They all dropped their heads. He then leaned back in his creaky desk chair, laced his fingers behind his head, and stared at the ceiling.

The boys fidgeted. After what seemed like an eternity, the chair came down with a resounding thud. All the boys jumped. The Booger leaned forward and began to speak. "Okay, I'm gonna tell you the conditions under which you can stay." There was a crescendo of "Thank yous" from the boys. "You'd better listen carefully. It won't be easy." He had their undivided attention.

"All right, number one." He picked up his legal pad and began to write. "You all will be on strict probation for the remainder of this school year. You mess up in any way, you're gone. Number two, all your weekend leaves until spring break are cancelled. Number three, you will serve detention every Saturday afternoon until spring break. Numbers two and three will be reviewed at spring break to see if we need to continue them further. Number four, you boys are exiled from each other for the rest of this school year. You are not to sit together, walk together, play together, study together for the rest of this school year. Don't even go to the bathroom and stand at the urinals and pee together. Are we clear on this?" They all nodded. "Okay that's it. Are you willing to stay on those terms?" They all agreed and thanked him again.

"Now, get on to class. Mr. Bledsoe, you will be taken into town today after school to see the doctor. Report to the infirmary,"

"Yes, sir. Thank you sir." Butch was more than relieved. The other four boys thanked him again.

"And one last ting," said The Booger, "your parents will be getting a letter from me explaining everything. What you tell them better match my letter." They all said that it would.

After the boys departed, The Booger went over to Headmaster Breckenridge's office and filled him in on the incident.

After lunch Lance, Tex, Shark, and Frog were discussing what had happened when Shark said, "You know, this reminds me of what my cousin Jess always says."

"And just what is that?" asked Tex.

"Well he always says, 'Don't never let your mouth write a check your ass can't cash.'"

The Senior Prom

"The best laid schemes o' mice and men
Gang aft a-gley."
  --Robert Burns

April 1950 at The Winslow School

The loud clanging of the bell on the wall above the phone booth sent what seemed like an electric shock through Tex's body and jolted him back into his own world. "I've got to run, Nancy June. The five-bell just rang."

"Aw, Tex. Just another minute. We've hardly got to talk any tonight." She was obviously disappointed.

"I know. Don just wouldn't get off the phone. But, anyway, we got the weekend worked out. I can hardly wait."

"Well, what do you think about me?" There was a sultriness in Nancy June's voice. "I've been waiting eighteen years for Saturday night. When I think about it, I get a funny feeling in my stomach. I hope you've got everything worked out on your end."

"I have. I sure have. I've thought of everything. I hate to hang up but I can't be late for study hour. It wouldn't do for me to get a detention and mess up this weekend. I'll try to get to the phone earlier tomorrow night."

"Bye, Tex. 'Til tomorrow night." Nancy June's voice was low and husky.

"Bye, Nancy June. And you know something? When I think about it, my stomach feels funny, too," Tex blurted out.

He hung up the phone and grabbed for the handle on the folding door. His hands were sweating and he was so excited from talking with Nancy June that it took him three attempts to get the door folded back. He ran up the stairs and down the hall to his room. He didn't even feel his feet touch the floor. The only thing he could hear was "Saturday night" running through his head over and over again. Just as he plopped down in his desk chair, the 7:00 o'clock study hour bell rang.

Tex's noisy entrance and heavy breathing interrupted Lance who was already at work at his desk. He looked up and commented with a touch of sarcasm, "On the phone again with Nancy June. That girl's gonna get you into trouble if you're not careful."

"That kinda trouble I can take," replied Tex as he pulled out his trig book and started his homework.

The roommates fell silent as they poured over their lessons. By 7:30 Tex realized that he had made no progress on his trig. None of the functions seemed to make any sense. He knew it was because thoughts of Nancy June, Saturday night's prom, and their "special plans" kept pushing the math aside. And this was only Tuesday. Saturday seemed at least a light year away. He knew that if he didn't get his mind on his lessons, he'd be in a deep hole before the end of the week. But he could not seem to force his thoughts away from what was going to happen. The anticipation made him warm all over. He had about resigned himself to the fact that he would be the only male virgin at UCLA come September. But he would be in a different category after Saturday night. He was finally going to get some trim.

He was about to burst. He just had to tell Lance. Lance wouldn't tell anyone. Since ninth grade, he's never known him to betray a confidence. Tex looked across the room at Lance engrossed in his English term paper. "Lance, can you keep a secret?"

"Why, of course," replied Lance somewhat annoyed by the interruption.

"Saturday night's the night, Lance. I'm gonna get some trim."

Lance swung round in his chair, the term paper forgotten. "You're gonna do what?"

"You heard me."

"Yeah, I heard you but I don't believe you. With Nancy June?"

"Well, who else?"

"Now, let me get this straight. You're bringing her to the prom, right?"

"Yes."

"Well, where are you gonna do it? You just gonna drag her under the bleachers after you fill her up with punch and cookies?"

"Why, of course not." Tex was becoming annoyed at his roommate's sarcastic tone. "Her dad's gonna let us use his car."

"Man, that's a new one on me. Mr. Davenport's gonna let you borrow his car so you can deflower his daughter in the back seat. Have you told him about this?" Lance was beginning to laugh.

"That's not funny, Lance." Tex was beginning to get a little angry. "I wouldn't do that. Besides I've got other plans. Things are all worked out."

"That's good. You seem so sure about it. Have you told Nancy June?" Lance began to chuckle again.

"You damn right I'm sure," Text replied angrily. "Who do you think helped me with the plans? Who do you think talked her father into letting us use the car? You think you're so blamed smarty. Well, let me tell you something. Nancy June's let me touch places I've never touched before and she likes it as much as I do. Saturday's gonna be a special night for both of us and I don't appreciate your making fun of it."

Tex's last revelation about Nancy June stifled Lance's laughter. His roommate was serious. "I'm sorry, Tex. I won't laugh anymore."

"You'd better not. And you won't tell anyone either, will you?"

"You know I won't."

"And you can just mark this down, Lance, old buddy. You're gonna have a different roomie come Monday morning."

"I'll remember that," Lance replied as they both turned back to their lessons.

* * *

As usual, Tex had a weekend leave with Frank Dunwoody in Sandersville. It was only fifteen miles away from Winslow's campus but it was so different from the boarding school atmosphere that it might as well have been on another planet. Tex remembered last September when Frank had invited him home with him for a weekend. Meeting Nancy June on that first visit had called him back on many subsequent weekends. A lot had happened since September.

They got into their tuxedos and Frank drove him over to Nancy June's house where he was to pick up her and the car. Both Mr. and Mrs. Davenport answered the door and invited him into the living room. They seemed like nice folks and Tex felt that they really liked him. They told him how nice he looked and asked about his school work and college plans. Nancy June was "not quite ready yet." Tex wondered why girls were seldom ready on time. He supposed it was their way of showing that they were in control or maybe they just liked to make grand entrances. He made a mental note to ask Nancy June about it sometime.

Tex got to his feet when he heard Nancy June coming down the stairs. He was not prepared for the dress. She had tried to describe it to him over the phone but he'd not paid close attention since he was not familiar with all the dress type terms. But when she walked into the room, Tex thought he was seeing something out of one of those movie magazines. He guessed the color to be ivory or something close to it. The bottom part was full but not so full that you couldn't dance close. From the waist up, it was skin tight and it seemed to push Nancy June's breasts upward. That, coupled with the low cut, revealed several inches of cleavage. Tex was visibly flustered. He had never been on a date with anyone with cleavage—at least not anyone who just had it hanging out like that. He knew he was staring but he couldn't help himself. "You sure look nice, Nancy June. Your dress is pretty, too," Tex somehow managed to stammer out.

"I'm glad you like it, Tex. You look good yourself," responded Nancy June.

"You both look wonderful!" exclaimed Mrs. Davenport as she jumped up from her chair. "Let me get my camera and take a couple of pictures."

She took three and would have taken more had Mr. Davenport not intervened. "That's plenty, Martha. These kids need to be on their way. Besides I'm sure they'll have some made at the prom."

Mr. Davenport walked them out to the car and handed Tex the keys. "It's full of gas," he said winking at them.

"Oh, please, Daddy," retorted Nancy June, "nobody would even think of using that old line these days." Mr. Davenport just chuckled at his humor and waved as Tex backed down the driveway.

As he drove to the campus, Tex kept looking at Nancy June. "Tex, you'd better keep your eyes on the road and quit looking at my breasts."

Tex blushed. "I just can't, Nancy June. I've never seen them look like that before."

Nancy June slid across the seat and snuggled up to his shoulder. "Well, you don't have to look so hard now. You know this is just a preview of coming attractions." Her words made him tingle all over. He was going to have a hard time waiting until intermission.

The dance committee had done a good job on the gym. All the crepe paper streamers gave it a festive air. However, all the colors in the rainbow could not cover up that distinctive gym odor of old tennis shoes, dirty socks, and sweaty bodies which seemed to permeate even the cinder block walls.

They danced almost every dance, had their picture made, and consumed several servings of punch and cookies. Along about 9:30 as they were dancing closely to a slow number, Tex whispered in her ear, "I'm jealous, Nancy June. I wish these guys would stop looking at your cleavage."

Nancy June whispered back, "They're jealous of you, Tex. And anyway, you shouldn't mind them having a little peek when you're getting ready to see the whole thing." Tex's whole body began to tingle again. Thank goodness intermission was close.

At 10:00 o'clock the band stopped playing and the lights came up. Intermission time. Most all the couples headed for the doors to spend the thirty minutes walking around the campus---and maybe sharing a kiss or two. Tex and Nancy June headed for the car which Tex had parked on the far side of the science building. The parking lot was in the opposite direction with a teacher usually on duty to discourage early departures or students using their vehicles for forbidden activities. As he helped her into the car, Tex noted that Nancy June seemed as eager as he was. His heart began to pound faster. He drove slowly without lights until they got safely off campus. So far, so good.

"Where're we going?' asked Nancy June as she snuggled up to his shoulder.

"You'll see," replied Tex trying to sound mysterious.

"Is it a nice place with lots of soft grass?"

"It sure is."

"I hope it's not far. I don't think I can wait much longer."

"No, it's not far," said Tex as he guided the car through the village.

When he got close to Hazel Green Cemetery, Tex cut off the headlights and turned in the cemetery's entrance road. "Oooooh Teeeex," squealed Nancy June. "How'd you ever think of a cemetery?"

"It wasn't easy—but I managed," Tex replied as he guided the car between the tombstones. Fortunately the moon was about full and only a few clouds in the night sky. Tex stayed on the main road that circled through the center until he came to an auxiliary trail running off to the right. He followed this path until it went over a small rise and ran among several large boxwoods. He stopped the car in the middle of the shrubs. The strong odor of honeysuckle from the nearby fence drifted through the car's open windows.

"This is just perfect," said Nancy June.

"It sure is," replied Tex. "You can't even see a car in this spot from the road in the daytime. And there's only a back pasture on the other side of the fence. I found this place when I was doing a tombstone project for American history."

Nancy June scooted over closer to him and put her arm around his neck. "I guess that just proves what my mother always says." She kissed him on the mouth.

"What's that?" asked Tex.

"A good education always pays off," responded Nancy June as she kissed him again.

Tex responded by dropping his head and kissing her cleavage. "I've been wanting to do that all night."

"And I've been wanting you to." Her voice was low and husky and sounded like Lauren Bacall. Tex was tempted to go into his Bogart impression but managed to restrain the urge.

Tex bent his head toward her breasts a second time but she stopped him with her other hand. "Let's don't get started here, Tex. I've got a blanket in the trunk."

"And I've got just the spot for it," replied Tex as he jumped out of the car and got the blanket. He led her up through the tombstones and around the little fences that marked old family plots. As they angled nearer the honeysuckle covered cemetery fence, the aroma from its yellow and white flowers became almost overpowering.

"We're not going to lay on a grave are we Tex?" Nancy June asked apprehensively.

"No, oh no," he answered. "There's a perfect spot up here in an unused section with a lot of soft Bermuda grass on it."

"Good. 'Cause I don't think I could do it on a grave. My mother says we should always have respect for the dead."

"I'm sure she's right," responded Tex although he was not much concerned at the moment with the dead or with Nancy June's mother. His thoughts were about him and Nancy June on that blanket.

They were now walking close to the fence with Nancy June being nearer to it. Neither had noticed the old Jersey cow who had her head stuck in amongst the honey- suckle nibbling some of the tender vine for a moonlight snack. Just as they got opposite the cow, a cloud passed over the moon. Startled by the sudden darkness and the arrival of two humans almost in her face, the cow responded with a long and loud "Moooooooooo!"

This scared the living daylights out of both teenagers but they responded differently. Tex stood rooted to the ground feeling his hair stand on end. In an instant he recognized that the sound had come from a cow in the pasture and was okay. Nancy June's response was just the opposite. She let out a shriek that could have been heard in Nashville. It crashed into Tex's right ear causing temporary loss of hearing. She whirled and ran back toward the car. Tex didn't see her go but he felt the vacuum caused by her sudden departure. In a few seconds, he heard another scream at the same time that he heard the crash. It sounded like a wreck in a junkyard with metal things banging together. There was a short period of silence and then the low moans began. These last sounds scared him more than the cow had. Nancy June was probably hurt.

Tex hurried toward the car and the moans. He was frantic. He'd never forgive himself if Nancy June were badly hurt. At that moment trim was the last thing on his mind. The cloud obliged by drifting away from the moon and giving him some light. It didn't take long to find her.

She had run headlong into one of those little iron fences around a family plot. The section she'd hit was bent inward. The force of the crash had snapped her body forward at the waist so that her hands were just touching the ground on the inside. Her toes just touched the ground on the outside. Her stomach rested on the pointed posts. Tex couldn't tell how far the posts had penetrated her stomach. He just knew he had to get her off. He slid one arm under her stomach on the inside of the fence and the other on the outside and lifted her straight up and off the fence. He put her feet on the ground and stood her up supporting her upper body with his left arm. Blood was coming out of the two puncture wounds in her stomach and making a dark stain on her dress. She continued to moan, "Ooooh Tex, my legs hurt. My stomach hurts."

"I know they do. Here, put your hands on the fence for a second and hold yourself up." She did and Tex took the blanket and refolded it into a long, scarf-like shape. He then wound it tightly around her body hoping it would at least slow the flow of blood. Then he picked her up and headed for the car. "Be brave, Nancy June, I'll get you to the hospital." Moans were her only response. He laid her in the back seat and told her to put her hands on her stomach and press down. Nancy June obeyed as if in a trance not really knowing why.

Tex drove as fast as he dared to the hospital in Sandersville. He stopped in front of the emergency room door and ran inside. His frantic explanation caused two orderlies to grab a gurney and race out to the car. They slid Nancy June out of the back seat onto the gurney and raced down the hall with her. She was still swaddled in the blanket.

Tex was left trying to explain what happened to the nurse in charge while she filled out a form. "I'll need to call her folks," he said.

"We'll take care of that," the nurse replied, "just give me their phone number and sit over there and wait."

"Can I see her?"

"No, not now. She's being attended to. You'll have to wait."

Tex sat down in one of the heavy wooden chairs and put his head in his hands. He wanted to run but he knew that wouldn't solve anything. He wondered what Mr. Davenport would do to him. He took a deep breath and resolved to take whatever punishment came his way. He dreaded the arrival of the Davenports. He did not have to wait long.

Their arrival was announced by the outside door's bursting open and banging loudly against the wall. Mrs. Davenport rushing in crying, "My baby! My baby! I want to see my baby!"

The nurse calmly told her that she did not think Nancy June's injuries were serious, that the doctor was with her, and that they could see her just as soon as he got through. This failed to slow her down. She ran over to Tex waving her arms and shouting at him to tell her what had happened. Finally, Mr. Davenport pinned her arms to her sides and forcibly sat her down. "Calm down, Martha! Your hysterics aren't helping anything! Let the boy speak!" Mrs. Davenport hushed and they both looked at Tex who stammered out an explanation.

"Well, you see, sir, it was intermission and we decided to take a walk in the moonlight through the cemetery and this cow scared Nancy June and she ran over a fence and the posts stuck in her stomach. Honest, sir, that's what happened."

Mr. Davenport looked at Tex and then at the ceiling. He began to run Tex's explanation through his mind out loud. "Walking in the cemetery, scared by a cow, ran over a fence."

"Yes sir, that's it."

"I swear, son, that's about the craziest thing I ever heard."

"I know, sir, but that's the way it was."

They all just sat looking at the floor. They made an unusual threesome. Tex's tux was all messy and wrinkled. Mr. Davenport had on an old pair of pants, his pajama top, and bedroom slippers. Mrs. Davenport wore a lacy nightcap covering a head full of curlers, a chenille robe over her nightgown, and fuzzy house shoes that made her feet look twice their normal size. No one spoke.

After about forty minutes, a man in a white lab coat carrying the bloody blanket appeared from somewhere in the bowels of the emergency room. Mrs. Davenport jumped up. "Oh, Dr. Maddux, I'm so glad you were on call. How is she?"

The doctor greeted the group, "Hello Martha, Melvin, and you must be Tex."

"Yes sir."

"She's going to be fine," the doctor announced.

"Did she say what happened?" asked Mr. Davenport.

"Said they were walking in the cemetery and a cow scared her and she ran over a fence."

"That's about what we got, too," responded Mr. Davenport still shaking his head in disbelief.

Dr. Maddux continued, "Either Nancy June was just tall enough or the fence was just short enough. Either way her hands and feet on the ground kept enough pressure off so that the posts did not penetrate through the abdominal wall. I put a couple of stitches in to close each puncture and gave her a tetanus shot. She should heal nicely although her knees and thighs are going to be sore. She bruised them up pretty good when she hit the fence. She did lose a little blood but the amount was minimized by Tex here when he wrapped the blanket around her." It was then that Dr. Maddux seemed to notice that he was carrying the blanket. "Here, I guess this belongs to y'all."

Mrs. Davenport spoke up, "Why, yes, I think that's one of the blankets that Nancy June keeps up in her room. Wasn't it fortunate that it was in the car, Melvin," she said turning to her husband.

Mr. Davenport's eyes narrowed as he looked at Tex. "Yes, Martha, real fortunate I'd say."

Tex could almost see the wheels turning in Mr. Davenport's head. He figured her father would have everything figured out in about thirty seconds. Her mother didn't have a clue. He wished the earth would open and swallow him.

Mr. Davenport turned to the doctor. "Doc, do you think anything else was broken?"

Dr. Maddux's eyes indicated that he understood just what Mr. Davenport was asking, "No, Melvin, I think everything else in intact."

"Thank goodness," replied Mr. Davenport.

"I'm going to keep her overnight just as a precaution. Y'all can go in and see her for a minute, but I've given her a shot which is going to knock her out pretty quick." He led them back to her room.

Her parents rushed to opposite sides of the narrow bed. Tex stood at the foot not sure exactly what to do. Nancy June was having trouble keeping her eyes open. She looked pale and tired. The gray hospital gown showed no cleavage. Tex noted the blood strained prom dress crumpled in the corner—just like his dreams, he thought. They kissed on her and rubbed her arms for a minute or two before her mother said, "Now you just go on to sleep and get some rest, honey."

Nancy June smiled and continued to fight off sleep for one last instance. "Tex," she said as she looked down at him, "thanks for taking care of me." Her eyes fell to and she was gone.

"You're welcome," he mumbled.

As they were walking back through the waiting room, Mr. Davenport said to his wife, "Martha, why don't you just wait here for a few minutes? Tex and I need to take a little walk."

"Well, Melvin, what am I gonna do?"

"Just sit right over there, Martha, and take care of the blanket," directed Mr. Davenport as he ushered Tex out the door.

Tex wondered to himself if Mr. Davenport was going to take him out and beat him up. But he dismissed that idea since he knew that he could run faster. They walked slowly neither speaking. When Tex could stand it no longer, he broke the silence, "I'm sorry, sir."

"I know you are. I know you wouldn't do anything to hurt Nancy June." He paused for several seconds before continuing. "Believe it or not, my boy, I was your age once and I expect my mind worked about like yours does now. I know it takes two to dance and I know you didn't put that blanket in the car. I guess one of my main jobs is to protect Nancy June from herself so, this seems to me to be a good time to make a break. You're going back to California in a few weeks and start college in the fall. Nancy June is going to school in state. Y'all will probably never see each other again. This only pushes the inevitable up a few weeks."

Deep down Tex had known it was coming but hearing it made him feel as if he'd been kicked in the gut by a mule. "May I visit her tomorrow?"

"No, I don't think so. You just need to say goodbye over the phone. I'll tell her it was my idea so she won't blame you."

Tex wanted to beg and plead and cry for one last personal touch but he knew he'd been given the final word. Both stopped. They had come back to the emergency room entrance. "Sir, I want to thank you for understanding. I guess I'll go on over to Frank's house."

"Do you need a ride?"

"No sir. He's waiting for me to call him to come pick me up. I'll just walk down to that booth on the corner and call."

"Do you need a nickel?"

"No sir. I've got one." As Tex was turning to go he saw that Mr. Davenport had his hand extended.

"Tex, I want to thank you for taking care of Nancy June. You don't know how much her mother and I appreciated it." They shook hands and for the first time Tex was able to look him in the eye.

He walked down to the phone booth, made the call, and sat down on the curb to wait. He buried his face in his hands. He felt worse than he'd ever felt before. And the worst thing of all: What was he gonna tell Lance come Monday morning?

(Excerpt from the EPILOGUE)

Whatever happened to:

Nancy June Davenport – She graduated that spring and enrolled in the University of Tennessee in the fall. She dropped out the following March and was sent away by her parents for an extended visit with an aunt in Oklahoma. The baby girl was placed for adoption.

Alford "Tex" Highsmith – Tex graduated and enrolled in UCLA where he spent one year. He transferred to a Jesuit college where he prepared for the priesthood. It is not recorded whether or not he ever got any trim.

Coon Dogs and Outhouses
Volume I
Tall Tales From The Old South

This first collection of his stories is part remembrance of a culture that is gradually fading, part recollection of lessons learned over a lifetime. Luke Boyd's matter-of fact style and clarity of detail are cut from the cloth of the oral tradition, which flourished in the rural South of his upbringing. He deftly places the hilarious story of chain saw-toting Phinos Ledbetter and his botched baptism at the East Fork Southern Missionary Baptist Church alongside the powerful memory of an uncle known by the poor tenant farmhands he served only as "The Jesus Doctor."

The author's characters are depicted so clearly and accurately as to leave the reader guessing which stories are fact and which are imagined. And whether the teachers in these tales are smudged with the dust of chalk or caked with the mud of the field, their lives and lessons are faithfully recorded here in the straightforward prose of Luke Boyd.

- ➤ Author: Lucas G. Boyd
- ➤ Publisher   TotalRecall Publications, Inc.
- ➤ Publication Date: 9/1/2008
- ➤ ISBN Paper Back: 978-1-59095-837-7
- ➤ ISBN eBook: 978-1-59095-838-4

Coon Dogs and Outhouses
Volume 2
Tall Tales From The Mississippi Delta

It was the Depression and very few areas were as economically depressed as the rural South. The road in front of our house was dirt (mud when it rained) and with no electric lights and no plumbing, we lived a bare and stark existence. There was no money to purchase entertainment so we made our own. Whether rocking on the front porch before bedtime or sitting around the kitchen table after supper, it was story time. Daddy was a storyteller and had a number of tales he told on a regular basis.

Stories flew thick and fast when visitors were in the house. With my uncles it was tales about the family or about people they grew up with. With neighbors I learned who had been caught making moonshine and who was stepping out on his wife. Much of my early education came from sitting on the floor off to the side during these sessions. I not only learned the stories, I also learned how to tell one.

- ➤ Author: Lucas G. Boyd
- ➤ Publisher   TotalRecall Publications, Inc.
- ➤ Publication Date: 10/16/2008
- ➤ ISBN Paper Back: 978-1-59095-839-1
- ➤ ISBN eBook: 978-1-59095-840-7

Coon Dogs and Outhouses
Volume 3
Tales from Tennessee

Some observations on life in general and people in particular as seen through a collection of articles, presenting skewed, off-beat, semi-serious, and sometimes amusing views of the world.

➤ Author: Lucas G. Boyd
➤ Publisher TotalRecall Publications, Inc.
➤ Publication Date: 10/16/2008
➤ ISBN Paper Back: 978-1-59095-839-1
➤ ISBN eBook: 978-1-59095-840-7

The Prodigal and Other Stories

Where did these fourteen tales come from? Some are true; some have an element of truth in them; four are chapters from a novel in progress; others just came into my mind and led me on a writing journey. But they are all fiction---more or less. That is not to say that some of these did not happen to some people at some time in some place. Nevertheless, they are still fiction.

Those who have read my earlier books probably noted that I tend to write in a light or humorous vein. Some of these pieces are just the opposite. One of my friends even accused me of "going over to the dark side." But a writer should be able to write about most anything as long as he/she "makes it interesting." Of course, you readers will be the judge of that..

- ➢ Author: Lucas G. Boyd
- ➢ Publisher   TotalRecall Publications, Inc.
- ➢ Publication Date: 4/28/20
- ➢ ISBN Paper Back: 978-1-59095-488-1
- ➢ ISBN eBook: 978-1-59095-501-7

www.ingramcontent.com/pod-product-compliance
Lightning Source LLC
Chambersburg PA
CBHW061621100726
47898CB00002B/758